Imperfect Strangers
By Mary Frame

This book is dedicated to all my murderinos.
You are my favorites.
SSDGM!

A portion of the proceeds from this novel will go to endthebacklog.org.
You don't have to buy this book to make a difference!
Go to endthebacklog.org to make a donation, see where your state stands on rape kit reform, and help eliminate the backlog of untested rape kits in the US.

A HUGE, HUGE thank you to Diely Pichardo-Johansson MD for your endless encouragement, spiritual guidance, and the medical advice contained herein.
(Any errors are purely my own doing to make Brent's condition and medical care fit my own fictional world and timeline.)

Chapter One

Bethany

I wake up in a strange bed with an arm around my waist.

Not this again.

It's a nice arm. Solid. Muscular. Strong, clean fingers.

I've done worse.

It may not be the first time I've woken up in someone else's bed, but it's the first time I don't remember who *someone else* is.

Disappointment wraps its cold fingers around my neck while my mind riffles through memories of the night before and my body absorbs the heat of the man cuddled around me like he belongs there.

I don't deserve the comforting heat at my back or the soothing sounds of breathing. Whoever he is, he's good. I'm an expert cuddler and this guy isn't even trying to press his morning boner into my back. That's like tenth level snuggling.

Reality blinks to life and slaps me in the face.

I went to bed last night alone. At Marc and Gwen's. I've been checking in on their apartment occasionally ever since they left the country weeks ago.

So who's the hottie draped over my midsection like he's got the right?

Muted grey light filters into the room as the sun forces its way through the concrete jungle outside. I turn my head to get a close-up look at my bedfellow and my heart stops.

I know him.

Well, I know *of* him.

Brent Crawford.

I'm snuggling with the tight end for the New York Sharks? The famous athlete? The gossip rag favorite? New York's sexiest bachelor?

Technically, this is his bed. He's Marc's brother and he does live here, but he's been MIA for months. Where did he come from? And why the hell is he spooning me?

For a few long seconds I don't move. I just watch him breathe and take in his nearness and slumbering good looks. My eyes linger over the defined angle of his jaw and the criminally long lashes that women pay hundreds to emulate. I turn my head forward and take in the corded muscles of the arms around me, apparent even in a relaxed state.

It is a truth universally acknowledged that any man in possession of such attractions is acutely aware of his own appeal and will use it to his advantage. Over and over and over again. With many, many women.

I used to be one of those women who didn't mind the game. Hell, I loved the game, but I've grown up. Men like this . . . they never really do.

I gotta get out of here before I do something dumb.

Oh so carefully, I wiggle to gauge his wakefulness. His grip tightens and he murmurs something unintelligible. Heart pounding, I shift and twist, taking my time and doing moves a contortionist would envy. Eventually I disentangle myself from his arms and slide from the bed. He's still breathing softly.

I am the queen of escape. A regular Houdini.

My half-naked victory dance is halted when I turn back toward the bed and find him sitting up and watching me, his expression a sleepy combination of confusion and interest.

His dark hair is rumpled and sexy and his eyes are a bright shade of blue so mesmerizing I almost rip all my clothes off and jump back into bed.

Plus, he's not wearing a shirt. The sheet only covers him from the waist down, exposing a chiseled chest and arms and . . . is that an eight-pack?

"Who are you and why are you in my bed?" His voice is rough with sleep, and a zing shoots straight to my lady bits.

Down, girl. "I'm not in your bed."

He rubs a hand through his sexy, tousled hair and frowns. "You were." Those vivid eyes narrow momentarily and then lighten. "You're Gwen's friend. Aren't you living at her apartment? Why are you here?"

My brain shuffles through possible excuses.

Watering the plants got really exhausting and I needed a nap.

Too lame.

I fell asleep while smelling your sheets.

Too creepy.

There's a ghost in my apartment and I can't sleep there.

Too unbelievable, even if it happens to be true.

"Oh, would you look at the time?" I glance down at my wrist. There's no watch there. "I . . . I have to go." I grab my overnight bag from the chair and bolt for the door.

I slept in only a tank top and panties.

3

He's totally getting an eyeful of my ass and cellulite and, ugh.

Doesn't matter.

"Wait." He shuffles behind me, pulling on his own clothes, but no one can get dressed and undressed as quickly as I can.

It's an art.

Before he's even made it out of the bedroom, I've pulled my pants out of my bag and I'm out the front door, buttoning as I race down the hall in the direction of the elevator.

The shiny metal doors close me into solitude and I take a deep breath, watching my panicked face in the mirrored walls.

As the elevator descends, laughter bubbles out of my reflection.

I can't believe I just ran away from the hottest man in the city. I mean, I knew there was a chance I would run into him. Gwen told me he would come back to New York eventually, but no one knew exactly when. I didn't think I would wake up with him in bed, though. That was definitely a surprise.

How did he not notice someone else sleeping when he got there? Sure, I have a tendency to huddle up into a ball. My friend Lucy would probably tell me it's because of some kind of internal psychosis or trauma, and she's probably right, but you'd think he would have turned on a light or something.

I guess I should be thankful he didn't bring someone home with him. That would have been even more awkward than this morning. Three-way no way.

I wipe a hand down my face with a groan.

Once I reach the bottom floor, I ask the doorman to get me a cab to Park Avenue. Might as well go straight to work instead of booking it all the way to Morningside Heights and back. At least I'm close enough to forgo the subway and I have my overnight bag with work clothes still stuffed inside.

As the car pulls away from the curb, I consider what I'm going to do now. Since Brent's here, I guess I won't have to check the mail and water the plants anymore.

I sink down into the seat of the cab.

But this means I'm going to have a much bigger problem.

How will I ever sleep?

~*~

"Beth."

My boss likes to shorten my name. I think because it's easier to bark. And just like a dog, when he barks, I come running.

"Yes, Mr. Crawford?" I stop in the doorway to his office.

"I told you to call me Albert." He's sitting behind his desk, shuffling papers.

"And I told you to shove it."

He almost laughs this time, covering his mouth and coughing to hide the sound before fixing me with a glare.

Everyone in the office is terrified of Mr. Crawford. Truth is, I am, too. Doesn't stop me from dishing his shit right back to him. I think he loves it, even though he threatens to fire me fourteen times a day.

The last assistant quit because he couldn't afford the amount of Xanax needed to deal with this guy. I have two things his former assistant didn't: boobs and a lack of tolerance for bullshit, no matter how important its source thinks he is.

Both are helpful when it comes to Mr. Crawford.

"How many more interviews do I have today?" he asks.

"Six."

He curses and mutters something under his breath.

"I could call the headhunter and see if we could spread them out, maybe reschedule a couple for tomorrow."

His eyes gleam. "You think so?"

I shrug. "Probably. But you have to promise not to fire me for the rest of the month."

"I don't make promises to pretty blondes unless we're in bed together."

"Keep dreaming, Mr. Crawford."

"Fine. You have a deal."

"I'll call over to the agency right now, sir." I smile sweetly before heading back to my desk.

I glance at the note stuck to the corner of my monitor.

Listen. Smile. Agree. Then do whatever you were gonna do anyway.

Marc quit unexpectedly and left the country with his girlfriend, but not before leaving behind inspirational quotes to help get me through my days. He stuck them in drawers, notepads, even one under my keyboard.

The former executive officer is going to be a tough act to replace—something Mr. Crawford is coming to appreciate, no doubt. But just because his son quit the company doesn't mean Marc stopped caring. After all, that's why his last act was to hire me.

Marc and his girlfriend Gwen are directly responsible for how I ended up in New York City with a new job. And how I ended up staying in Gwen's haunted apartment. Which turned into crashing periodically at Marc's apartment.

I finish scheduling the remaining interviews for the week with the headhunter and then it's nonstop for the next few hours.

I have my own work to get to, plus I'm the buffer between Mr. Crawford and, well, everyone else.

Grace from accounting sends me payroll documents for restaurant-chain commissions that need to be signed by the end of the day. Eric from marketing emails reports about potential new kitchen suppliers and aggregate sales data along with a long message begging me to organize them for Mr. Crawford. Lana from HR sends me a pop-up asking if I can compile some of her data about employee satisfaction into a color-coded file.

I have a small spreadsheet obsession. Okay, it's a large spreadsheet obsession and everyone knows about it and uses it to their advantage.

And through it all, I don't think about Brent Crawford and his snuggling abilities.

Nope nope nope.

Okay, so I try not to, but since my boss is his dad, it's not exactly easy to forget him. Or his azure blue eyes. Or his naked chest. All of which make me think of hot nights on a Caribbean beach with lots of exposed skin. I really hope he doesn't ever come to the office. He could melt off my clothes with a smile, along with every other female's in a ten-thousand-mile-radius, which means he's dangerous to my general health and well-being.

This is a no-man zone for the foreseeable future. Out of service. Nothing to see here. Well, unless the man in question is interested in a serious adult relationship, and I doubt Mr. Hottie McHotpants famous football player man is available for anything other than a quick hookup.

Hot men don't have cold beds.

I'm going to run into him eventually. Maybe it would be good to meet him with all my clothes on. I'll be completely professional and eloquent. I'll be drinking tea out of one of those fancy porcelain cups with a dainty handle, pinky up, speaking with a crisp British accent and saying things like "Tally ho!" and "Are you taking the piss?" and "Beg your pardon" and —

"Beth!"

I jerk in my seat and my recently refreshed cup of coffee spills all over the front of my bright white blouse.

Then again, maybe eloquence is out of the picture.

"Yes, Mr. Crawford?"

"My son's in town. We need reservations at Gilt for tomorrow night."

"On it."

I glance down at the soggy brown fabric clinging to my chest.

Tomorrow, I'm wearing black.

Chapter Two

Remember, tomorrow is promised to no one.
–Walter Payton

Brent

"A funny thing happened on our way through the Alps. Gwen convinced me to snowboard again for the first time in fifteen years. Will I die? Probably. So my final words to you are this: stop being a dickbag and call me. Also, I know you'll have to come home soon since training is starting. Will you check on Gwen's friend Bethany? She's working for Dad. I want to make sure she isn't too traumatized by the experience. She doesn't know anyone in New York. Send me an email or something if you can."

My thumb hovers over the call-back button.

I want to talk to Marc. Tell him everything. But I've always leaned on my brother.

Story of my life. He's the strong one. I'm the needy one.

He's traveling with his girlfriend. I'm holed up in a waiting room alone.

He's happy, and he deserves it, and I refuse to ruin it for him. Also, if I'm being completely honest with myself, slithering jealousy wiggles around in my stomach every time I think of Marc.

He got the girl.

I'm still alone.

9

Before I can decide to not call Marc back for the fortieth time, the decision is taken from me.

Dad's calling.

"I need you to be here by three."

"I'll get there as soon as I can." My brother had the right idea, leaving the country. He no longer has to deal with Dad's crazy. Only I get the honor at the moment.

"I need you to help me win over Jim Sinclair, owner of the HouseMart chain stores. He's a big Sharks fan."

"Sure. Whatever you need," I respond absently. I have my ball cap pulled low over my head and sunglasses over my eyes, but I'm getting the side-eye from an elderly gentleman sitting across from me in the waiting room.

I do not want to be recognized.

It doesn't help that the only TV in the waiting room is currently on ESPN and they're running an interview I did last season and highlighting all my major pass plays and touchdowns.

I hunch down even further.

The nurse calls my name from the door. First name only, but still, the old man gives me a sharp look.

I stand from my seat.

"Listen, I gotta go but I'll see you soon." I hang up before he can respond and then follow the nurse down a narrow hallway with bland beige carpet and stark white walls.

She smiles and makes idle chatter while checking my weight and blood pressure. Then she tells me the doctor will be right in and I'm left alone in a sterile room, my hat and glasses perched on the side table.

I'm here to face what I've been avoiding for months.

Hypertrophic cardiomyopathy. A seemingly random string of letters, but when you put them all together, it means my heart could stop beating at any moment.

Just like Mom's.

"It's good to see you again, Mr. Crawford." Dr. Richards shakes my hand. She's probably midfifties with dark, wavy hair pulled back from her face and warm brown eyes.

"No offense," I say lightly, "but I'm not sure I could say the same."

It's not that I don't like my doctor. She's the best cardiologist in the city. But after she hit me with my initial diagnosis, I was angry. And she was the only one I could take it out on.

Luckily, she didn't hold it against me. Even when I phased from denial to anger and then straight back into denial.

She smiles and meets my eyes. "I know it's not an easy thing to deal with. No one wants to make these kinds of decisions, but I'm glad you're here. And I'm here to help you find the best possible solution."

I nod.

She taps on the tablet in her hands. "You had a 2-D echo the last time I saw you and we discussed surgical options. Are you wanting to talk about treatment?"

"Yeah . . . and I'm out of beta-blockers."

"They've been helping the dizziness and palpitations during activity?"

I nod. "They were. I haven't been exercising with the same level of exertion since the season is over. But I've been taking them anyway. I still do some exercise. Just not as intense. But I'll have to go back to work next week."

Organized team activities — or OTAs — and minicamps. Voluntary, but I signed up to help.

She puts her tablet down on her lap. "I know we've discussed this previously, but I still recommend a complete halt to all strenuous activities."

I remain silent.

11

She sighs and picks up her tablet again. "Are you still having the same side effects we noted before?"

I swallow. "Yes." The beta-blockers have a side effect. In addition to easing my chest pains and shortness of breath, they cause impotence. Only an idiot would be angry about not being able to have sex when death is on the line, but it is one more thing to add to the numbing dissonance of my life.

Also, I'm pretty sure I'm at least a little bit of an idiot.

"Okay. Can we talk about the surgical procedure?"

"If I have the surgery, will I be able to play after? Can you give me a bill of health for the team?"

She takes in a slow breath and I know I won't like her answer. "I can't guarantee anything. The risks are relatively low, one to two percent risk of death and three to five percent risk of further damage to the aortic valve. But there are major risks with every surgical procedure. As far as playing after . . . I don't know. We'll have to assess that once the surgery is completed."

My head is shaking as she talks. "I can't risk my career."

"We could at least implant the defibrillator. The recovery is less significant and it would likely prevent the sudden death associated with your condition."

Sudden death. Once again I'm reminded of the potential fallout but my mind shies away from delving too deeply into the thought.

We've discussed the defibrillator before. It's like an implanted resuscitator. If my heart stops, it delivers a jolt to restart it. They implant it under the skin.

"I don't know." I run a hand through my hair. "Everyone would be able to see it." There would be too many questions from teammates in the locker room. What would the coaches think? They would think I'm a liability. It could ruin my career. No one knows about this except the person in the room with me right now.

"The best chance of returning to play is the myomectomy surgery," she says gently. "But I strongly recommend you at least get the defibrillator if you're planning on returning to work."

I nod, my heart thumping dully in my chest. Blasted organ. "Before we do that, can I get another test? Just in case the echo wasn't entirely accurate. Something more detailed might show more. You said sometimes athlete's heart can emulate the condition."

"That's true, but with your family history and the thickness of your septum . . ." She trails off, watching my probably bleak expression before nodding her assent. "I can order an MRI for you."

I shift in the hard seat. "Thank you."

"I'll give you a prescription for two weeks," Dr. Richards says. "We should be able to have the test scheduled by then. Have you thought about talking to someone else about all this?"

"Like who?"

"Family. A friend. Maybe a therapist or the team physician?"

No. I signed a release form at the end of the season stating I was healthy.

Lies.

"I'll think about it."

~*~

I make it through the pharmacy without being recognized. Then I drive to Midtown to get to Dad's

13

office, keeping my sunglasses on and hat pulled low the entire time.

My life for the last three months has been like this — like living with dark shades on. Everything is tinged in grey. Food tastes bland. My thoughts are muddled. I don't sleep well.

With the exception of the other night.

I stumbled home late, so tired I fell into bed without even realizing there was someone else there. I should have turned on the light when I got home. But I was exhausted. Another lovely side effect from the beta-blockers.

And then I slept better than I had in months.

Maybe it was the result of having a warm body snuggled against me. I had nearly forgotten the world-altering miracle of a good night's sleep.

She smelled like wildflowers and mint. Tart and sweet.

I didn't even realize she was there until the sun was rising and I was curved around her like a spoon, all soft skin and sweet smelling, like it was the most normal thing in the world.

Her blonde hair curled out of control and I could only see the curve of her cheek and a full lower lip. If I could get an erection, it would have happened then. The bitch of it is, my libido is as strong as it ever was . . . I just can't do anything about it.

She must be Bethany, Gwen's friend who's supposed to be living in her apartment. Why was she there? Marc said she's working for Dad.

Maybe I'll see her today.

I pull off the sunglasses for a brief moment just to get past security, waving at Stan before shoving them back over my eyes and getting on the elevator crammed with businesspeople tapping or talking on their phones.

On the top floor, halfway down the hall, my steps slow.

I yank off my shades so I can see her in full color.

She's here.

Standing in the door to Dad's office, her back to me.

I recognize the curly hair. Even though there's been an attempt to tame it back into a bun, a few strands escape the abuse and curl at the nape of her neck and around her ears. My eyes slide down to her petite yet curvy figure. A dark grey collared blouse shows off her trim waist and a black skirt hugs her thighs to her knees.

She's lot more put together than she was when she scrambled out of my bed yesterday. Interest flares low in my belly, just like it did yesterday morning.

Frustration flickers through me.

The fact that she bolted like she was on fire did nothing for my insecurities.

I know I'm not ugly. I'm an attractive guy by all accounts. It's not like women don't want me. A lot of women want me; they're just always the *wrong* women.

Her words get louder as I approach and I almost don't believe what I'm hearing.

"You can't go anywhere right now." Her voice is firm, full of authority. "I rescheduled these interviews per your request. The agency is going to pitch a fit. You can't bail on me now."

No one talks back to Dad.

"Who's the boss here again?" he bellows from inside his office, using the same tone from when we were kids, the one that sends children crying and grown adults running for cover.

But she doesn't run. Instead, she straightens, chin lifting. "Someone who refuses to take his job seriously."

I stop a few feet behind her, entranced.

"You're fired," he says.

"Ha! You can't get rid of me for another three weeks!"

"We didn't shake on that deal."

"Oral agreements are binding in the state of New York." She crosses her arms over her chest and smirks.

"Did you say oral?"

She laughs and then groans, slapping a hand to her head. "You are the most frustrating man in the whole world."

He's quiet in his office for a few seconds and then his voice is softer. "I told you I have dinner plans with my son."

"I'm the one that made your reservations. For five. It's three."

There's more silence. I can't see his face from here, but something makes Bethany crack.

She grunts. "Fine. I'll let you leave if you can take an extra interview tomorrow."

There's muttered grumbling from beyond the wall.

I move closer until I'm standing behind her, a few feet from the desk situated outside of Dad's office.

"And another thing, you have to bring me one of those chocolate cakes from that new dessert restaurant everyone's talking about—Decadence or whatever." She pauses, watching him. "And you can't leave until you've reviewed the marketing analysis I emailed you this morning."

"You're a pain in the ass, you know that?"

"Don't act like you don't like it." She turns around and runs right into me.

I saw her coming. I could have moved, but I didn't want to.

I grasp her shoulders when she stumbles. "Sorry."

She looks even better from the front, her button-up top exposing an enticing peek of cleavage and the stumble revealing a glimpse of a bright red, lacy bra.

16

I glance back at her face quickly to avoid getting caught staring.

Her eyes are on my chest. They flick down, then back up to my face. Her cheeks flush pink. Her mouth pops open, then shuts again.

Stifling a laugh, I release her shoulders. She was totally checking me out.

I grin.

So the whole running away thing wasn't because I'm disgusting or have a sign on my head that reads *Fear ye all who enter here*. It's nice to know I still have it, even if I can't do anything about it.

I call out over her head. "Hey, Dad."

"Brent, give me just a minute. A beautiful woman is making demands I can't refuse."

"No problem. I'll wait out here. Bethany, right?"

She hasn't moved. Her mouth is ajar. She clicks it shut and straightens, lifting her chin.

Her smile is small. Polite. "That's me. Nice to meet you." She sticks out her hand for me to shake, like we weren't wrapped up around each other less than forty-eight hours ago.

I grasp her fingers. Her grip is small but firm and she releases my hand quickly.

So that's how it's gonna be.

She moves over to her desk, sitting primly in the chair, focusing on her computer.

I sit in the guest chair just outside Dad's door, facing her.

She's clicking away at a breakneck pace, completely absorbed in whatever she's working on.

I clear my throat and she turns more of her back in my direction. Is she trying to ignore me?

"I have to say I'm impressed."

"Hmmm?" She flicks me a glance and keeps typing.

"My father doesn't listen to many people. He likes you."

She snorts. "You call that liking someone? He's a menace."

"You're still here, so that's something."

"Only by sheer force of will."

I laugh. The sound is rusty. I don't think I've laughed out loud in months.

The smile she tosses me is cheeky.

She's interesting. And attractive. And a complication I don't need.

"Do you want some water or something while you're waiting?" She shuffles some papers on the desk.

"Actually, yeah." Her words remind me . . . I need to take the pills I just picked up. I wave her off when she starts to stand. "I can grab a bottle from Marc's mini fridge. Is that where you guys still keep those things?"

"Yep. Still trying to find someone to take over who will put up with the giant baby in there." She jerks a thumb toward Dad's office.

"I heard that," Dad calls.

"Good," she yells back.

Chuckling I head down the hall to Marc's old office.

If I didn't know better, I would think he never left. There are still files scattered around and a few pictures on the corner of the desk. I pick up a paperweight with a capital letter *F* attached to a mini bomb. I bought it for Marc a few years ago, for when Dad made him want to drop the *F* bomb.

Even with the clutter, it feels empty. Abandoned.

I miss my brother. He was always there, cheering me on, helping me when I faltered, and listening when I needed it.

I grab a water bottle and swallow the meds, the pills going down harshly despite the cold water. I put the drink down and pick up an old family picture resting on the corner of the desk. Dad and Mom are sitting with us kids on their laps. Marc's with Dad, no more than three or four, and Mom's holding me. I was just a baby. Mom's laughing, and even Dad is smiling.

Memories of Mom have faded with time. I was only ten when she died. Marc is always talking about her distinctive laugh, but I can't remember what she sounded like. I only remember her scent, like lemons and sugar. She loved to bake.

After she died, Dad withdrew into his work and Marc was the one who was always there for me. Always at my games, always making sure I had everything I needed to succeed. Now he's out in the world, enjoying it. The thought makes me happy and a bit nostalgic. Now it's my turn to take care of Dad and the company. I've always relied on Marc. Now I need to be someone other people can rely on.

The task is a weight pressing me down. I can barely face my own problems. How can I help anyone else?

My gaze is drawn to Dad in the photo, smiling and happy. I haven't seen that smile since before Mom passed. Maybe I should tell him about my medical issues. Maybe it will snap him out of work mode—make him realize there's more to life than business deals and photo ops.

"Hey, sport. You ready?"

"Yeah. I'm ready." I put the picture back and follow Dad out of the office.

As we're heading down to where the car will pick us up, we pass a bunch of people heading in the opposite direction.

"They're all waiting to bug Beth until I leave. Bunch of sissies, all of them." Dad waves a hand, not bothering to lower his voice as a thin, pale guy in glasses darts by, his eyes averted.

19

For so long, Marc was the buffer between Dad and the rest of the staff. It appears Bethany has slipped into the same role.

"So things are going well then? With Bethany."

He waves a hand. "She's fine."

Fine. Quite the compliment, coming from him. Nothing about her tits or physical appearance. Maybe he's growing.

Or maybe it's just her.

Chapter Three

Did Satan change diapers? What kind of father was he?
–Georgia Hardstark
My Favorite Murder episode 73

Brent

The restaurant perfectly matches Dad. Upscale. Lots of men in business suits. The walls are all dark wood paneling and there's some kind of esoteric structure behind the bar that changes colors periodically. Throw in the expensive bourbon and it's everything Dad loves in one convenient location. The name is even appropriate. Gilt. The definition of opulence.

Or, add a *u* and you've got the feeling every parent inscribes into their children from birth.

All I can think when I look around is pretentious bullshit. The only women present are arm-candy blondes.

I never wanted to be part of this world. I left all this to Marc. I just want to play football. My place is on the field, not in the boardroom.

And now my place is nowhere.

"Have a scotch with me." Dad slaps me on the back as I slide into the bar where we're going to wait until our reservation time.

"I can't. Training."

"Ah. You've got great willpower, Son. You're a credit to your team. They're lucky to have you."

"Thanks, Dad."

He's smiling and happy. Again I consider telling him everything. It would be nice to have someone to talk to.

"Now tell me." He nudges me with an elbow. "You getting a lot of tail in the off season? It's a good thing you got rid of that Bella girl. It's no good having to deal with a ball and chain when you're a single, good-looking guy, amiright?"

Aaand he's back. "I didn't get rid of Bella, she broke up with me."

He blinks at me as if he can't possibly comprehend why I would admit to something so enfeebling and then waves a hand dismissively. "Whatever." He turns the subject to a few business partners he wants me to meet, some people who are investing in the new expansion project he's been working on for the past year.

"Marc told me all about it," I say. Marc did the majority of the work on the project. Before he quit.

"Right. Well, it's a good thing I have a real man now to help me front the company. Let me tell you my plans."

And off he goes, and everything is "I" and "me" and what *he's* been working on. No mention of Marc. He doesn't even say his name.

It's a defense mechanism. It has to be.

It's clear to me it bothers him, how Marc left. The fact that he won't even say Marc's name proves as much. But the old man will never admit to being upset, or to something as "feminine" as missing one of his own children.

It's the Crawford way. Deny, deny, deny. Don't let them see you go soft.

When I was a kid, it was always, "shake it off," and "use your emotions on the field."

22

Like it's never okay to express any feeling other than anger or aggression.

~*~

"Jim, come meet my son," Dad calls out across the bar. We halt our way to our table as Dad's acquaintance makes his way over.

I recognize the name, if not the face. Jim Sinclair is the owner of HouseMart, the home supply giant. Didn't Dad mention he wanted to get our products into their stores?

Jim is a middle-aged man with thinning hair and an expensive suit. We shake hands and then he introduces the woman with him.

"This is my daughter Angela. Angela, you know Albert. And this is his son Brent."

I shake Angela's hand. She's a petite blonde with ultra-white teeth and a demure black dress. Her handshake is firm.

We make small talk and then Dad invites them to eat with us.

Crap. Dinner definitely won't be over until late.

An inkling whispers through me before we get to the booth. A premonition, if you will. This was planned, probably for a reason I won't like.

My suspicions are confirmed as we're walking to our table. "I wouldn't mind finding a way to join our two empires," Dad mutters to me with a wink and a nudge in Angela's direction.

He's maneuvered it so Angela and I are sitting side by side, across from our dads.

And there it is.

I'm being whored out by my own father.

Great.

Maybe now would be a good time to tell him I'm impotent.

My jaw clenches. Not that the state of my cock even matters. I'm fine. It's *fine*.

As Jim's drones on and on about some merger or acquisition or whatever, Angela clears her throat and leans in my direction. "He's really into scalable business strategies and leveraging things," she whispers. "Pretty much anything involving business jargon that sounds impressive but is actually useless."

"You're not into it?"

"Not really. But I pretend to be for my dad." She shrugs. "This stuff is important but he never—" She cuts off and glances over at our fathers.

"He never what?"

She shakes her head. "It's nothing."

Dinner is served and it's actually not a bad time.

Angela is nice enough. She's smiling and listening to our fathers talk, a look of perfect interest and understanding on her face while she quietly sips her wine. Every part of her is pressed and smooth, not a hair out of place.

Not like Bethany's haphazard bun with the escapist curls.

I take a long drink of cold water. None of that matters. I can't be thinking about women. Too many other things on my plate. Not to mention the fact that my lower half is useless. Not something that's necessarily bothered me much over the past few months, considering my other concerns . . . but it kind of bothers me now.

I wish the night were over already. Exhaustion is wrapping languid fingers around my body, making my thoughts fuzzy around the edges.

As it is, I'll have to go back to the office to pick up my car—I left it in the lot next to the building. I pat my pocket surreptitiously to make sure I have my keys and realize I'm missing something else.

My pills.

I left them in Marc's office.

"Brent," Jim interrupts my thoughts. "I hear you're involved in a lot of charity work. Angela is involved with the Ladies Auxiliary right now, raising money for children of active-duty military families."

They're all staring at me, waiting for a response. "That's really great."

"We're having a charity auction in a couple of weeks." Angela smiles at me. "A lot of the sponsors are big Sharks fans."

The eyes of my table partners land on me like a three-hundred-pound barbell. I can't say no. "I would love to help." That's not a lie. It's a worthy cause. But this isn't about the charity. It's about manipulating me into spending more one-on-one time with Angela Sinclair.

"Something that won't take up too much of your time," Angela says. "Maybe a signed football? I'll give you my number."

Dad claps me on the back and answers for me. "That sounds great."

Chapter Four

*A lot of love at first sight is like the first time you meet a
sociopath.*
–Karen Kilgariff
My Favorite Murder episode 66

Bethany

After Mr. Crawford and Brent leave, the rest of the
day hums with activity. There's a mad dash to rearrange
schedules and appease ruffled feathers since Mr.
Crawford left early. In addition, a good chunk of the day
is spent making sure everyone in the building has what
they need from Mr. Crawford's office. Which is a lot,
since there's a mass infiltration as soon as he exits the
premises.

On top of that, I have to deal with a missing pallet in
the Jersey warehouse, act as a buffer between payroll and
a distraught salesman yelling about a missing
commission check, and answer the never-ending phone
line with calls from investors, buyers, and anyone and
everyone else in the kitchen supply industry.

By the time I'm leaving, the sun is setting on another
day. I wave goodbye to Stan the security man and then
begin the trek home, which involves three different
subway changes.

It's not too bad, though. The subway isn't as
frightening a place as I always imagined it would be.

Back home, there's nothing like it for public transportation. I've had to adjust.

And it's not just the subway. Everything here is so different from home. Out west, everything is large and open. A mortgage for a five-bedroom house costs the same as my teeny tiny apartment. Manhattan Island is tightly packed, over a million people in a twenty-two-mile radius. Reno has a population of four hundred thousand over a hundred-mile radius. New York smells like greasy food and exhaust. Nevada is all clear mountain air and sagebrush.

I'm surrounded by all of these people, but I know almost no one.

All my best friends still live back home. But at least I'm three thousand miles away from my mother. Even though her long tentacles of guilt manage to reach me from afar.

I've got my key in the lock when the neighbor's door opens.

"Hey there, Bethany. Work late?"

Dammit. So close. "Hey, Steven. Yeah this whole adulting thing is bullshit."

Steven is close to my age, maybe a couple years younger. He's tall and trim and has dark hair and a mustache. Not a hipster handlebar mustache, or a giant state trooper 'stache, more like a fluffy dead caterpillar that ends before the curve of his lips. It's totally a porn 'stache. He's friendly, if a bit odd. And hard to get away from, one of those people who just wants to chat and won't shut up and you have to edge your way out of the conversation.

Also, I'm pretty sure he's in a cult.

"We're having ornithology club tonight. Did you want to come over? We're going to come up with a new name for the group."

See? Cult. Who belongs to a club about birds? In New York City, no less. What are they studying, pigeons? Hard pass. Besides, the only person I've seen showing up for these meetings is a guy named Adrian with dead eyes.

"You know, it sounds like so much fun, but I have plans." I've got the first lock open. I stick my key in the dead bolt.

"Grandma Martha made crab cakes," he says, like that will change my mind.

Martha's cooking is terrible. She brought me cookies when I first moved in and I think she used salt instead of sugar. Gwen was always going on about how great Martha's cooking was, but that ship has sailed. She has dementia and Steven moved in a couple months ago to help her out.

"Aw man, bummer I'm going to miss it."

"We have a new member in the club. Natalie Furmeyer."

"That's . . . nice. Tell Martha and all the cul-ub members I said hi!" I finish unlocking the door and slide in, shutting it behind me before he has a chance to say anything else.

Now on to my big plans for the night.

Twenty minutes later, I'm in PJs, eyeballing my dinner choices: frozen meal or questionably aged takeout leftovers? How does one really decide? Before I can choose between explosive diarrhea now or explosive diarrhea later, my phone rings.

Ted.

"Tell me something exciting," he says in lieu of a greeting.

"Did you know Ed Kemper, a.k.a. the co-ed killer, has voiced over five hundred audiobooks? There you are, enjoying a nice relaxing listen to *Flowers in the Attic*, and really it's the voice of a serial killer."

He groans. "You and serial killers. You have a problem. Gimme something less murder-y, please. Anything exciting happen lately that doesn't involve death and dismemberment?"

"I woke up in bed with Brent Crawford yesterday morning."

He snorts. "Right. So really, who'd you bang?"

"I didn't bang anyone. I had to go over to Marc and Gwen's to sleep—"

He cuts me off with a groan. "Not the poltergeist crap again?" He heaves an exaggerated sigh. "Bethany. Ghosts aren't real. Neither is Santa, the Easter bunny, or trustworthy old men in positions of authority."

I gasp. "You've ruined Christmas. And the Electoral College."

"You're going to ruin your vagina."

"I told you, there was no banging."

"I've heard that story before."

"Because it's true," I mutter. Back home it was always easier to let my friends believe I was clinging to my wild and randy youth rather than admit the reality. I didn't want to go home. I still haven't told them the full truth, and I probably never will. "Look, I haven't actually gotten legitimate sleep in like a week. I was desperate and exhausted. Not horny. I woke up and he was there and I bolted like a total loser who doesn't know how to socialize."

"Like Lucy?"

"Exactly. Except I don't have the science smarts, only the zero social skills. Then he came to my work to see his dad and witnessed another lovely firing from our favorite CEO."

"How many times has Mr. Crawford fired you now?"

"I lost count around twelve. He doesn't mean it. He's just ornery. I think it's because he's lonely."

29

Seriously. I found him once lingering in Marc's empty office. He said he was looking for a file, but there was a hitch in his voice and a sheen in his eyes. He tried to hide it by yelling at me about the dust, but I saw it anyway.

"He's lonely so he fires you?"

"He's like a kicked puppy. He growls to protect himself, but inside he just wants love and maybe a doggie bone."

Ted snorts. "You mean you want the bone."

"Hell yeah I want the bone, but I swear I didn't sleep with Brent. I'm keeping it in my pants, just like I told you I would."

"Fine. I believe you. But I still think you're tripping about the ghost thing. Ghosts aren't real. It's probably rats or noisy neighbors or something."

A siren sounds outside. I move a few steps into the living room and shift the corner of the drapes with one finger. Lights flash in the distance, moving away and down the street. "Maybe." I let the curtain drop. "I asked Steven and he hasn't heard anything odd."

"Steven! I love that guy. How's the bird cult?"

"Ugh, don't even get me started. He invited me over again tonight for their meeting."

"Are you gonna go?"

"What? No. Are you insane?"

"Bethany, you need to get out. You need to make new friends, even if they are a bit culty and weird. I know it's going to be hard to find someone as amazing and talented and good-looking as I am, but I'm three thousand miles away. I can't meet all your needs."

"No one can," I murmur, more to myself than to Ted.

"I gotta go. It's our twenty-three-month anniversary. Tony's taking me to dinner."

"Puke. Do you guys have to celebrate every month?"

"Yes. We're adorable. Don't be jealous. Actually, do be jealous because I kind of enjoy being envied."

I laugh. "You're such a bitch."

We hang up and I finally decide to eat the questionable takeout. While it's spinning in the microwave, I gaze up at the ceiling and think about what the hell I'm doing here.

I originally decided to move to New York to escape my mother and all of her issues, which had somehow morphed into mine. But it hasn't turned out like I thought it would. I fantasized about making all kinds of friends, spending nights out on the town, really enjoying life without stress.

Instead, I've been working myself ragged and coming home alone to an apartment I can't sleep in. And I'm still getting sucked into Mom's problems. I thought she would be better without me but it's getting worse.

Ted's right. I need to find friends. A shoulder to cry on. Someone to distract me from my problems.

The most pressing one being my inability to sleep through the night.

Maybe there is a plausible explanation for the weird noises — one that won't freak me out and make me think of every horror movie I've ever seen. And maybe tonight will be quiet.

A door slams somewhere down the hall and I nearly jump out of my skin.

Then again, maybe not.

Chapter Five

Never trust a beautiful person.
–Georgia Hardstark
My Favorite Murder minisode 74

Bethany

A bang reverberates through my dreams, jolting awareness into my sleep-addled brain. The overhead light is on. I blink drowsiness from my eyes, my tired mind rushing to register what's happening around me.

My nose is numb with cold. It's freezing.

The window is open.

It's March. There was a nor'easter last week. I did not leave the window open before I fell asleep.

Was I sleepwalking? Not something I've ever done before.

I rush to the window, clicking it shut and twisting the lock. Then I glance around my living room, rubbing warmth back into my arms. I blink at the illuminated ceiling light and then over at the switch on the wall.

Someone turned it on. Someone opened my window.

This is not normal. This is not my imagination. This is not rats. Rats can't open windows or turn on lights. They don't have thumbs.

My heart thumps in my chest, trying to break out of the cage of my lungs.

There's an overnight bag on the small chair in the corner, left there from all the other nights I've bailed and gone to Marc and Gwen's. Can't go there now, but I can't be here either.

My instincts push at me.

Get out.

I grab the bag from the chair, then my purse from the counter. I rush out into the hall, locking the door behind me.

Now where to? I pull out my phone. I don't know anyone and I'm not staying with Steven.

I check the time. And I've only been asleep for an hour.

Motherfucker.

A hotel is out of the picture. I paid my rent and then I had to pay Mom's utilities for the month, which barely leaves enough for food for either of us.

There's only one place I can think of to stay for free.

I splurge on an Uber to Park Avenue. What choice do I have? The office stays open all hours for late work nights.

"Stan. Can you do me a solid?"

Stan's eyes are kind and concerned. "What's happening, Ms. B? Shouldn't you be home in bed? Or out at the disco or whatever you young people do these days?"

"I'm having a little issue with my apartment. I need somewhere to sleep. Just for tonight. So I was going to use the couch in Marc's old office. Please don't tell anyone," I beg.

Maybe more than a night since this crap isn't getting any better. If anything, it's getting worse.

"I don't know, maybe I should call Mr. Crawford. I'm sure he would put you up somewhere."

"It's just one night, Stan. I promise, I'll talk to him in the morning."

I'm not telling that old bastard anything.

Stan finally relents and I head up the elevator.

The office is quiet and full of shadows. I pass my vacant desk and groan at the voicemail light, shining in the dark.

Not thinking about it till tomorrow.

Marc's office is almost exactly like my apartment, except bigger. There's a mini fridge and a couch and he has his own private bathroom with a shower.

I put my bag on the chair and glance around the dim office. I don't come in here very much. A picture on the desk catches my eye. It's Marc and Brent with their parents. Their mother is laughing, and even Mr. Cranky Crawford is smiling. Brent still has those dimples. I put the frame back down next to a prescription pill container.

What's this?

B. Crawford.

Some kind of football injury? I put it back down. None of my business.

In the bathroom, I smile at another sticky note from Marc. He left this one on the back of the door.

If you're hiding from Dad in here, just picture flushing him down the toilet.

After peeing, I get out my stuff for the morning. I'll have to get dressed and sneak over to the office before Mr. Crawford gets here. Shouldn't be too hard. He's notoriously late.

I'm pulling my mousse can out of my bag when I hear something.

Noises out in the office.

I almost groan out loud. Not here, too. I can't deal anymore.

But it doesn't sound like anything supernatural. There's a cough. The shuffle of footsteps.

34

The cleaning crew is done for the night. No one would come into Marc's office right now. What if someone followed me from my apartment?

No. No physical person could be in here. Stan wouldn't let them in. Maybe it really is a ghost. Maybe I accidently opened a hellmouth and now the spirits have awakened and will follow me everywhere I go and I'll have to find the graves to salt and burn the bones and escape their evil clutches.

I grab the only weapon I can find. The can of mousse I just put on the counter.

Great, Bethany, what are you going to do? Style the intruder to death?

Maybe I can throw it as a distraction and then make a run for it.

I fling open the door, give some kind of strangled karate yell and toss the can at the dark figure hulking around the desk.

They catch it smoothly in one hand.

It's not a ghost or bandit of any kind.

It's Brent.

"Hey." He sets the mousse down and holds up both hands in a gesture of innocence. "It's just me. I forgot something. What are you doing here?" He glances at the can he just set down. "And did you just throw hair product at me?"

I sag against the wall, a soupy mixture of relief and embarrassment. My chest heaves from the adrenaline and my skin prickles in mortification. I sink to the floor, taking deep breaths to calm myself. I hold up a hand. "Just give me a second."

I am such an idiot. Of course he came back for those pills. I *just* saw them and read his name on them. It makes sense he might actually need them. What is wrong with me? The lack of sleep is making me lose my mind.

"I . . . thought you were a bad guy," I say finally.

"I kind of picked up on that." He moves closer and crouches down in front of me. His blue eyes are dark in the dim light, and his brows are creased. "What are you doing here so late?"

"I'm just," I shrug with attempted nonchalance, crossing my arms over my chest, "you know, working really really hard for your dad."

A brow lifts.

I look up at the ceiling for inspiration. "I'm protecting the company assets."

The other brow rises to meet it.

"Cleaning the," I glance around, "counters?"

He nods, the corner of his lips twitching in amusement. "It's possible you're the worst liar I've ever met."

I slouch even lower, defeated. "Ugh. I know. It's so inconvenient. My life would be so much easier if I could spew crap like everyone else."

"Besides, no one works in their PJs. Are you sleeping here?" He eyes my pants.

I'm wearing my *Supernatural* pants. They have little Sam and Dean faces all over them.

This is not embarrassing at all.

I cross my legs. "Why do you ask?"

He counters with another question. "Is there something wrong with Gwen's? Is that why you stayed at our apartment the other night?"

I can see he's not going to let this go.

Sigh.

"If I tell you, you can't laugh. And you have to promise to believe me."

"We've already established you're a crap liar."

"I know, but it sounds crazy. Even to me and I'm the one experiencing it." I rub a finger over a seam in the carpet and glance at the windows. The city lights twinkle back. When I find the courage to bring my gaze back to

36

Brent, he's watching me. His gaze is open and full of concern. I can't believe he cares. Although, his eyes also look a little red and hazy. It's late. He must be tired and now he has to deal with my crap and he's pretending he gives a shit so he can go home to a supermodel or something.

Better to just blurt it all out before I lose my nerve. "It started a few weeks ago. I woke up to strange sounds in the middle of the night. Nothing scary, just a weird tapping sound. It would be fine for a night or two and then start up again. Then it got worse. Louder. Banging in the walls. At first, I thought it was just, you know, normal noises for the city. Thin apartment walls, et cetera, but when I mentioned it to one of my neighbors, he never hears anything odd and they live right next door. I emailed Gwen. She never had anything like it when she lived there. I haven't been sleeping. That's why I was staying at Marc's most nights, but only when the noises were bad. But then tonight . . ." I bite my lip.

"It's okay. You can tell me." He puts a hand over mine.

I stare down at our hands. He's so warm. His fingers are long and his palm is wide. He has strong hands. Capable. I don't think I've ever had such large hands over mine.

I swallow. Brent isn't dangerous. I know his brother. Gwen even dated him for a few months. He's safe. "When I went to bed, everything was fine. Then I woke up with the light on and the window open. I can't sleep like that. I prefer solid darkness and I get cold in ninety-degree heat. Someone else had to have opened my window and turned my lights on, but no one was there. I panicked and came here."

He doesn't say anything and I risk a glance at his face. His blue eyes are intent and serious. He's not laughing, so that's something. "Maybe there's a plausible explanation."

"There probably is. But I'm not really feeling like I want to find the answers in the dead of night by myself."

"Have you tried talking to the super?"

"Yeah. He thought maybe it was air in the pipes or something. He had it checked out and said the pipes are fine and I must be crazy."

"Your super said you were crazy?"

"He didn't use those words per se, but he sure looked at me like I belonged in Bellevue."

He cracks a smile. "It's late. Come stay at Marc's. You can have his bed." His hand tightens over mine.

"Bed?" The word is almost a squeak.

"Yeah. You know. Sleep in a real bed and not on Marc's couch in a dusty office."

"That's a really nice offer, but . . ."

"But what?"

His gaze is innocent, his voice sincere. He wants to help me.

Can't be trusted.

"I'm not going to sleep with you," I blurt.

He frowns. "I just said you can sleep in Marc's bed. I'll sleep in mine. No hanky-panky."

I snort out a laugh and my nerves ease somewhat. "Did you just say hanky-panky?

He sits back, removing the connection of our hands. "What's wrong with that?"

"What are you? Eighty?" I laugh, teasing him. I slap my knee. "Okay, I'm not worried about you making the moves now. No real playboy uses the term hanky-panky. Phew, thanks for that."

"I'll have you know I get all the hanky—I mean women I want."

Sheesh, someone's sensitive. He must get the fragile ego from his father. Why is it that the most beautiful people are always the most insecure?

I roll my eyes. "I'm sure you do, Casanova." I pat him on the shoulder. "I'm not doubting it, I'm just saying I don't want to be one of the many."

"Well you don't have to worry about it." He stands and grabs his pills from Marc's desk with a hard snap. "Ready to go?"

I tamp down the simmer of disappointment. Why would I expect anything different from a guy like him? He's just another hot guy whose giant ego can't take a tiny joke.

Chapter Six

Toxic masculinity ruins the party again.
–Karen Kilgariff
My Favorite Murder episode 44

Brent

Within minutes we're driving back to the apartment and I'm mentally berating myself.

Why did I snap at her for the hanky-panky comment? Granted, there's been zero hanky-panky in my recent past, so I'm a little touchy about the issue, but I normally don't let those things get to me. Having a potentially lethal heart condition is a lot more serious than sex.

What is it about her that gets under my skin?

And why did I invite her to stay with me? What was I thinking?

I was thinking Marc told me to check on her. She's an obligation.

Then again, maybe it's because she's a distraction. A very attractive one. Even with her funky pajamas and makeup-free face, she glows with vitality and moves with an innate sensuality that draws me like a fish to a lure.

These thoughts aren't helping.

It's just one night. She'll be gone in the morning.

"What kind of car is this?" She's stroking the armrest and eyeballing the interior like she wants to make out with it.

I yank my gaze back to the road because her roaming hands are giving me dirty thoughts. Thoughts that will lead nowhere. Maybe since I can't actually have sex, I'm becoming overly focused on it.

Also still feeling a little emasculated about our last conversation.

She was just teasing me. It shouldn't bother me. It wouldn't bother me if I weren't dealing with manhood issues already. And probably even less if I hadn't just spent the night with my father.

"It's a Porsche Panamera."

"It's so pretty. Can I drive it?"

"The only other person who's driven Carla is Marc."

"Carla? You call your car Carla?"

"Shhh, she'll hear you." I pat the dash.

"Yeah and she's gonna be pissed you gave her such a lame-ass name."

"What would you call her?"

"Pepe le Hot Stuff," she says without hesitation.

I laugh and a bit of the tension in my body releases at her words. Anyone who wants to call my car Pepe le Hot Stuff cannot be taken completely seriously.

It doesn't take long to reach the building in Greenwich Village because of the late hour. I hand my keys off to the parking attendant and then wave to the doorman as we pass through the lobby. Bethany keeps pace behind me at an angle, her body turned and hunched behind mine. She's clearly trying to hide but only succeeding in drawing more attention to herself.

"What are you doing?"

We reach the elevator and she shuffles to keep herself from view of the front desk. "They'll see me."

"Does it matter?"

41

"I guess not. But aren't you some kind of celebrity? You don't want the paparazzi catching you with some nobody who can't even put on real clothes." She tugs on the hip of her sleep pants.

The elevator opens and we step inside. I press the key for the tenth floor. "I don't really care what the gossip rags say. I've been through worse."

She scoffs as we move up. "Everyone says that, but it's a lie. I'm sure there's something you wouldn't want everyone knowing."

I almost choke on my own tongue.

Once we're in the apartment, I toss my keycard on the table in the spacious entryway and hold the door open for her.

She walks past me, kicking her shoes off onto the tiled floor and leaving them by the door like she's been here a hundred times. Which, I guess, she has.

"I guess I don't have to show you around." My gaze runs over the open floor plan, the white walls with original prints from expensive artists, the luxury furniture. Is this all an elaborate ruse for her to stay here instead of her shitty apartment in Morningside Heights? It wouldn't be the first time a woman has taken advantage of my wealth.

Maybe not. I did invite her here, after all. She would still be at the office if I hadn't happened to stop by.

She turns to face me, wringing her hands. "This is weird, isn't it?" She bites her bottom lip. "I'm so sorry. I've basically taken over and ruined your night. It's late. I'll just use the facilities and get out of the way."

"It's fine, really. I'm glad I'm able to help. Just let me know if you need anything."

She nods and disappears with her bag down the hall.

All my thoughts about her being a gold digger fly away. Her distress at taking advantage was too genuine.

If she really wanted something from me, she'd be a lot more brazen and a lot less eager to flee.

I change into sleep pants in my room. Sitting on the edge of the bed, I breathe in the faint scent of Bethany that still lingers on the sheets. Wildflowers and mint. The fact I slept better the other night than I have in months has to be a fluke. It doesn't mean anything. Maybe it's because I was back in my own bed after being away for so long. That has to be it.

Curious about how my houseguest is faring, I find her in the guest bathroom, digging through drawers, toothbrush in hand.

"Can I help you find something?" I ask from the doorway.

"Oh, hey." Her eyes flick over me and then immediately fly to my face. "I was just looking for toothpaste." Her cheeks flush pink.

I'm not wearing a shirt.

May have been an intentional choice. And it was worth it. She's totally checking me out.

My chest puffs slightly.

It's been a while since I've felt attractive enough to enjoy attention. My job is basically to work out every day and be in tip-top shape but . . . after Bella dumped me and then Gwen rejected me for Marc, my ego has been bruised.

I catch her checking me out again when I hand her the toothpaste tube, forcibly swallowing the grin threatening at my lips.

Her cheeks are still tinted pink. She uses the tube, hands it back without meeting my eyes and then starts brushing with vigor.

Bethany is different from most of the women I've known. Not only is she a terrible liar, everything she thinks is immediately reflected on her face. It's kind of fascinating. She clearly likes what she sees and yet she's

43

trying to hide it. Why? Because she thinks I'm some kind of man-slut?

She spits, then meets my eyes in the mirror. "How are you tan in March?"

"I did some traveling after the season ended." I shrug and lean against the doorframe. "Needed to get away for a bit."

"Where did you go?"

"Turks and Caicos."

"Oh, right. Turks and Caicos."

She doesn't exactly roll her eyes and say poor little rich boy, but I swear it's what she's thinking when she turns her face and keeps brushing.

When she's done, I hand her a small towel so she can wipe her mouth. "So when did all this stuff with the apartment start? You said a few weeks ago, but you moved in a couple months ago, right?"

"Yeah, I moved in after Christmas. Things didn't start getting weird until last month."

"Was there anything else happening to explain the noises? Construction? Change in ownership? New neighbors?"

"No. But I don't really know my neighbors anyway, except Steven and Martha, so I wouldn't know if any were new or old or whatever. And I've asked Steven if he ever hears anything. He's a heavy sleeper and Martha has hearing aids, so they were no help. "

"Hm." I speak before thinking. "What time do you get home tomorrow night?"

"Probably around seven. Depending on how long Mr. Crawford wants to torture me. Why?"

"How about I pick up dinner and meet you there at seven thirty? I bet between the two of us, we can figure this thing out."

"Dinner?" She's frowning.

Why is she frowning?

44

You should absolutely leave her alone. You are no good for anyone right now.

But I want to help.

And it's more than generosity of spirit prompting my actions. The past few months have been a lonely stretch of bleak days, one after the other. Bethany is like a spark in the darkness. It's the only explanation for why my tongue keeps misbehaving. "What, you don't like food?"

"I love food. It's just that . . . dinner sounds really date-y to me."

A surprised chuckle escapes me. "This isn't a date. I'm helping you."

"Why are you helping me?"

"Do you have anyone else?"

She frowns. "Not really. But why do you care?"

What a great question.

Why do I care?

I shrug. "Marc told me to look out for you. You need help. And I'm here. I promise it won't be date-y. We can just be friends." I give her my best, most charming smile, the kind that makes the fans cheer and the press snap photos like they're at a royal wedding.

She gasps. Her eyes widen and she covers them with her hands. "Oh, no. If we're going to be friends, you can't do that."

"Can't do what?"

Her fingers are still hiding her eyes. "Smile with your face! Those dimples are lethal. What's next? Are you going to cuddle some puppies?"

I laugh and tug her hands from her eyes. "Hey. I kind of have to use my face to smile, you know."

"Yeah, well . . . it's kind of shitty of you."

Now I can't stop smiling. I'm still holding one of the hands I pried away. "I could use a friend right now, to be honest."

45

I think I've laughed more since I met Bethany than I have in the last year.

"You're right." She bites her bottom lip. "I could use a friend, too. I don't know anyone here. The only parts of the city I've seen are on the subway route between Park Avenue and Morningside Heights."

I gasp in feigned shock. "You've been here for months and you haven't seen the city?"

"Afraid not."

"That needs to be rectified immediately. So, see, we would both benefit."

After a slight hesitation, she nods and sticks out her hand. "Friends."

We shake on it and I ignore the way her slim fingers slip over mine, warm and solid, a shot of lust going straight down my stomach . . . and settling like a clogged drain.

"Friends."

~*~

When I walk past Marc's room the next morning, it's empty, the bed neatly made.

The kitchen and living room are quiet, but there's a clean cup left next to the coffee maker with a note.

Dear friend,

Thanks for the toothpaste and letting me ride in Pepe. You're swell.

B

I make my coffee with a smile.

Sleep wasn't great last night. It's not just being in my bed that made the difference.

After I shower, there are a couple hours until I have to meet with my agent, Roger, and then get my tasks sorted for the day.

I pick up my old football and pace the living room, half watching a sports network on TV.

The leather is soft and worn beneath my fingers. I toss the ball in the air and catch it. I feel . . . better. Lighter. Maybe the meds are kicking in.

I drink my coffee and prep a few meals for the week. I have to get back on my diet for the season. The irony of the action isn't lost on me, but if I defer from my habits too much, I might crack. Technically, I'm not required to return to work until mid-July, but there are minicamps coming up and I agreed to help with training. It's good for morale, getting to know the new players and reconnecting with the returning veterans. Nothing brings men together like sweating and bench pressing and tossing around the old pigskin.

After I've done all my chores for the day, I head uptown to see Roger. A few hours later, I'm leaving Roger's office for a press obligation when my cell rings.

"Hi Brent, it's Angela Sinclair," a breathy voice says. "We met the other night at dinner."

"Right. How's it going?"

"I'm great. I was wondering if it was possible to bring the signed football you promised for the charity to my apartment sometime this afternoon. If you're free."

I glance at my watch. After the interview, I have to meet the director of Marc's kids club and there are a few extra things I want to pick up before I meet Bethany at her place tonight.

"I can have someone bring it by. Text me your address."

"Oh. Right."

There's a long pause. Long enough that I'm about to check if she's still on the line or if I've lost her, but then she speaks. "Sounds good. I'll text you now. Thanks, Brent."

She hangs up and I pull the phone from my ear and frown at it. No doubt Dad will give me shit for ducking this setup, but I don't have time to dwell on the conversation because I need to get across Manhattan for my next meeting.

Three hours later, I've just parked outside the kids club in the Bronx. I have a meeting with the director for the annual charity baseball game.

It's important to my mother's legacy that this event goes off without a hitch. She started the program before she died. She always had a soft spot for children in need. The kids club for underprivileged Bronx youth gives them somewhere to go after school and provides a ton of enrichment programs, from sports to art to music.

I'm getting out of my car when my phone rings again.

"Hey, Dad, what's up?"

"Brent," he barks. "You need to get uptown to bring Jim's daughter the football."

"Um, I'm kind of in the middle of something. I'm having an assistant drop it off later."

"That's unacceptable. Jim is my friend."

What does that have to do with anything? Frustration lends sharp edges to my words. "I don't have time this afternoon for a silly errand."

"It's not a silly errand. Jim is an important investor. For his family, you will make the time."

"But Dad —"

Click.

I stare at my phone.

He hung up on me.

I groan and my head falls back against the seat.

Ten minutes later, I *really* don't have time for Dad's shenanigans.

48

"Our event planner is inaccessible," Rosemarie tells me as soon as I'm sitting in her office inside of the kids club.

"Inaccessible?" I ask.

"She's in Japan, trying to find her mom."

"Japan?"

Rosemarie sighs and pulls her wire-rimmed glasses off, cleaning the lenses with her shirt. Her brown eyes are tired when they meet mine. "June's mom has dementia. Periodically she leaves the country without notice and flies back to Japan on her own. Normally, June would get a call from the authorities when they find her mom wandering around, but this time no one can find her. So June had to leave. I haven't been able to reach her since she took off last week."

"And there's no one else who can take over?"

"We can't even get into her computer to see what she's taken care of so far. And once we have that, we still need more hands. We barely have enough in the budget for the people we already have."

I nod. "Okay. I might have a solution for getting into the computer. I'll work on the rest, I promise."

I leave a still frazzled Rosemarie behind.

Maybe I can borrow an assistant from Roger. I already do that a lot. Or one of the IT people at the company. I know there was a computer tech who volunteered to set up a website for the kids club, a friend of Marc's.

Angela lives in the East Village. I'll have to run by my apartment in Greenwich before heading to her place. Bethany's apartment is in Morningside Heights. This means I'll have to drive to the other side of Manhattan Island and back during rush hour.

I sigh.

I'm going to be late.

Since I don't have Bethany's number, I call the office to reach her.

"Mr. Crawford's office," she answers, her voice crisp and professional.

"Hey, it's Brent."

"Oh, hey." There's a pause and then, "Did you need to talk to your dad?"

"No, I actually wanted to talk to you. I'm going to be a little later than I thought."

Chapter Seven

A champion is simply someone who did not give up when they wanted to.
–Tom Landry

Bethany

I'm home, sitting on the couch slash bed and staring at a box resting on the faded brown ragtag coffee table.

The package was delivered by a courier—some college-aged kid with long hair who reeked of pot. All he could tell me was it was "on behalf of Brent Crawford."

What could it possibly be? A new toaster? A puppy? A sex swing? I'm still coming up with ideas when my phone dings.

Google alert.

I have Mr. Crawford's name in my notifications so I can be prepared in case of a PR emergency.

I pull it up, expecting the normal article about a merger or deal or what have you, but the article is mostly about Brent.

He was just spotted going up to the penthouse of one Angela Sinclair of the HouseMart fortune.

Is this why he's going to be late? The article goes on to mention that Brent and Angela were also spotted recently at dinner with their parents. I frown at the final sentence. *Does this mean he is going to propose!?*

It's not like I have or want any claim on Brent. He owes me nothing. If anything, this article is a good reminder about why getting involved with hot, rich, famous dudes is a bad idea.

Besides, he's the son of my boss. Bad ideas all around.

I'm not giving up my cookies to just anyone. I'm saving them for someone worthy.

Except . . . it's been so long, I think my cookies have crumbled.

I glare at the box like it's the one jumping from one girl's apartment to the next and being all hot and flirty. Dumb box.

I need a distraction. I pick up a new bottle of nail polish and the Ann Rule book I started last night about Ted Bundy.

It's almost eight when there's a buzz at the door.

Brent.

I click the button to let him in the building and toss the book in a drawer. A few minutes later there's a knock.

He's fast.

"Hey." I try to be professional, but the word comes out more breathless and sultry than I intended.

"Hey."

I'm still wearing work clothes, skirt, blouse, but no shoes. I wanted to avoid repeating pajama time with Mr. Sexy Grin. His eyes linger on my newly painted pink toes before flicking back up to my face.

A tingle of excitement follows his gaze from my toes up the rest of my body.

Did he seriously just check me out after leaving his latest floozy's apartment?

And did I seriously just enjoy being objectified?

I clearly need to work on my antihoochie behavior.

Or I need to get laid.

"You brought pizza." Focus on the food, not the hunky man in the doorway. It's hard not to be intensely aware of him towering over me. His broad shoulders fill the space, body tapering down to a trim waist, and no, I'm not going to stare at his junk.

Eyes up, Bethany.

"Best pizza in the city." He lifts the unmistakable white box in his hands with a gentle shake.

I open the door wider and step back. A whiff of his cologne teases me as he walks by. Something expensive that makes me think of hot breaths and tangled limbs.

Dammit.

"Do you want anything to drink? I have water and . . . more water." Good. Remind him I'm a broke-ass loser. That's great.

He grins, opening the pizza box. "Water sounds good."

The pizza almost smells more delicious than him. Almost.

"That looks amazing. I'm starved." I hand him his water and pull out a couple of chipped plates from the cupboard. I take a bite and groan. "This is the best. Pizza is my fourth favorite food."

"Fourth favorite?" His brows lift. "What's one through three?"

"Tater tots, chicken nuggets, and mac and cheese."

He barks out a laugh. "What are you, five?"

"Only emotionally. I think it's why those are my favorites. It's like comfort food. Reminds me of my childhood." Before Dad died and Mom went to shit. "What about you? Something super mature like lobster tails and caviar?"

"Hardly. Pizza is probably number one."

"Probably?"

"I don't eat a lot of processed food. I keep a pretty rigid diet because of football. It's the off-season, so I splurge occasionally."

"Ah."

Lifestyles of the ultra rich and healthy. He probably has a personal chef. The thought makes me glance around in embarrassment. I have a miniscule apartment with worn furniture and dirty windows.

He follows my gaze and glances around the small space. "I've never been in here before."

"Never? Not even when . . . ?"

When he was fake-dating Gwen who ended up with his brother, Marc?

Awkward.

"I walked Gwen up to the door once. After a game." He frowns down at his plate.

I know why he's frowning. He wanted her. She didn't return his feelings.

I heard the whole sob story from Gwen herself. I wonder if a guy like Brent really cares, though.

"Have you heard from them since they left?" I ask.

"Yeah, Marc calls and sends me emails whenever they have access. They're happy. Gwen's even trying to get Marc to snowboard again." He smiles at me, and now . . . he doesn't look terribly heartbroken or anything. Which makes sense. I mean, he can have anyone he wants. He probably found solace in the arms of a different model. Or Ms. Rich Angela Sinclair.

The thought makes my stomach turn. So I won't think about it. We're just friends. "Marc's going to snowboard again? That would be amazing. That's a huge deal."

He has scarring over one side of his face from a snowboarding accident when he was a teen. Hasn't been on a board since. Before the accident, he might have gone pro, according to Gwen anyway.

"I'm really proud of him," Brent says, still smiling.

I clear my throat. "So, what's in the box?" I gesture to the delivery sitting on the coffee table.

His smile widens. "It's a camera for the front door."

"Camera? How much do I owe you?"

He waves me off. "Nothing. It was cheap."

"How much is cheap in rich man land? Because I think your definition of cheap and mine are going to be vastly different."

"Well, technically I bought it for Gwen. It's still her apartment and we can leave it here or she can take it when her lease is up. So really, it's not even for you. Besides, everyone has one of these nowadays. It looks and functions like a doorbell, but there's a camera inside."

"Well, if everyone has one, and it's actually for Gwen, then I guess it's okay.

"They're pretty cool. There's an app you can download to your phone and then you can see activity and view live feeds at any time."

"Seriously? That's fancy as fuck."

He nods. "Just like a spy movie."

"Okay, but I get to be the ninja with all the skills and ass-kicking excitement."

"What do I get to be?"

"You're the arm candy."

He laughs. "I guess I'll take what I can get."

He helps me clean up after dinner and then gets to work setting up the camera.

Inside the large package is another smaller box. "Here. I got this for you, too."

I turn it over to read the front. "Is this . . . a night-light? It has Sam. And Dean. And Castiel! You got me a *Supernatural* night-light?" My eyes snap to his.

He's smiling. A small flush colors his cheeks. "I thought you might like it. You know, because of the pants."

My mouth pops open. "You noticed my pants and went out of your way to find me a matching night-light?"

"It's no big deal. I'd do it for any friend." He clears his throat and walks toward the front door.

I hug the box to my chest. "You're a really good friend, Brent."

And a friend you will stay.

I try to help him, but after giving him the Wi-Fi password, he insists it won't take much time and he hardly ever has the opportunity to do this kind of stuff. So I sit on the futon and get some work done while he goes out into the hallway, working on the front door.

Once he's finished, he helps me download the app on my phone and set everything up.

Then he shows me where he's installed it on the door. It only needed one screw so there's no damage to upset the landlord and the screw hole can be easily filled when it's time to move.

"Can you set it up on more than one phone?"

"Yeah, up to four."

"Can you link it to yours, too? Just in case."

"Are you sure?"

"Yes. That way, if you don't see me leaving for more than two days, it's time to make sure I haven't been murdered and stuffed in a suitcase."

He grimaces. "No murder allowed on my watch." He taps on his phone, setting up the feed, before he walks over to get the jacket he left on one of the chairs.

"Before you go, take a look at this." I walk past him to the coffee table where I've left my laptop open. "I've been tracking when the incidents occur to see if there's a pattern." I turn the screen in his direction so he can see the spreadsheet I've been working on.

56

"That's actually really impressive." His eyes scan down the color-coded sheet.

"I've tracked the occurrences by day and time."

"What did you find?"

"There's more activity on the weekend and on Thursdays. Tonight is a typically quiet night. Thank God."

He nods at me but his mouth tilts down and there's a crease between his brows. "I'm not sure I'm comfortable leaving you alone."

"I'll be fine. Nothing bad has happened, except for the sleepless nights. I can handle noises. I've been here for three months and I'm still alive. Besides, what if it's all in my head? Maybe I've cracked and now I have split personalities and I'm gonna go all crazy and you'll see me on video running around the halls covered in animal skins and peanut butter."

He laughs. "That's always a possibility. One I hadn't really considered, actually, but now I think it's burned into my brain. Where would you get the animal skins?"

"That's the part you're worried about?"

He laughs again, shrugging his large frame into the sleeves of his jacket. "Yeah."

"I'm sure there's some subway rats I could catch."

He groans. "Oh God, no. Don't go there."

We both smile and then there's an awkward moment where he's glancing around to make sure he didn't leave anything and I'm trying not to think about the fact he's probably leaving here to go back to Angela Sinclair's penthouse apartment. She probably doesn't need cameras on her front door. She has a legion of doormen and personal security guards, maybe a giant Doberman with a pink collar named Gertrude.

"What an asshole," I grumble.

"What was that?"

"Nothing," I say quickly. "I, uh, be careful driving so you don't end up in a sinkhole."

"That doesn't sound like what you said.

"I'll . . . walk you to the door." I practically shoo him toward the exit. Which is literally two feet away.

Good job, Bethany.

He stops at the door and turns to face me. "I'll call you tomorrow to check on things."

"You don't have my number."

"I do. I put it on my phone when I was setting up your app."

"You stole my number?"

"Don't make it creepy. We're friends, aren't we?"

"I guess we are."

Since there's no way we could ever be anything more.

Chapter Eight

Believe me, the reward is not so great without the struggle.
–Wilma Rudolph

Bethany

The text comes through early the next morning.
Still alive?
Brent might be a super player hottie McHotpants supremo, but at least he's also considerate. He is actually a great friend so far. I don't know any other famous athletes who would take the time out of their glamorous schedule to schlep downtown and help a little peon like me. And then text the next day to check in.
I tap out a return text.
Sort of.
Not ready to skin the rats yet?
Maybe by tomorrow.
It's nice having a guy friend.
A guy friend who walks around without a shirt and makes me pant after him like a basset hound. He's got, like literal acres of golden skin. Who has golden skin in March? The kind of people who fly off to Turks and Caicos at a moment's notice, that's who.
This guy is so out of my league.
And it doesn't matter, because why would he go for someone like me when he's got someone like Angela Sinclair?

Angela Sinclair, who not only comes from a family worth a bajillion dollars, but is also petite and blonde and perfectly put together in every photo I can find online — because I googled her. For reasons.

Shoving thoughts of prim heiresses aside, I focus on my current task. It's Saturday. No work but lots to do, including laundry in the creepy basement of my building.

It's almost three when I get the call.

"Hey, Mom," I answer.

"Hey there, baby girl."

She's drunk. I can tell in only five syllables. It's the word choice and the cadence, the slight slur she's trying to hide. I can still hear it even though anyone else would miss it. It's noon back at home.

Drinking already? I want to ask, but I bite my tongue. She'll get defensive and we'll fight about it and tomorrow morning she won't even know she talked to me, but I'll remember it forever.

"I can't pay the power this month," she says.

"I already paid your bills." Thank God the mortgage is paid off.

I've had to pay the utilities and taxes for the last two months. She drank her whole bank account by the second week of the month.

I moved out so I wouldn't have to deal with this crap, and for the first few weeks, it was better. Or maybe she just improved at hiding it. At least when I lived there she would maintain for a few months at a time. Having me around made it a little harder for her to go totally crazy. Now she has free rein.

But it's going to get better. *She's* going to get better. That's what I've been telling myself for the past decade, anyway.

"Oh. Well I need money for food," she says.

"I'm not sending you money." We've played this game before. She'll use anything I send her for more booze and definitely not food. I learned the hard way I can't give her money directly. If I'm going to help, I have to send the funds straight to the vendor. "What do you want? I can call the store and have some food delivered. Tell me what you need."

She's silent for a few long moments, and I can feel her thinking through the connection of three thousand miles, trying to figure out a way around me. "I'll call you back."

She hangs up and I stare down at the phone.

I can't let her problems ruin my day. I've had enough. It's the number one reason I took a job on the opposite side of the country. Along with having nothing else to do, really. All my friends are married and busy being happy and I was sick of being the pathetic friend. The one with the pity invite. The one who can't make it past a first date.

I've been waiting for my own Prince Charming, and since he wasn't showing up in Reno, I went to New York City.

And then there's Mom. I have to let her go. The realization slammed into me a month before Marc offered me the job here.

I had come home early one morning and she was awake and drunk. She called me a dirty whore, a no-good piece of shit, and other things that I've tried to repress.

She's not normally a mean drunk, but once in a while, she hits the point of no return and twists into a monster.

But she never remembers it once she's slept it off.

That was my final straw. The moment I realized that I can't change her. Nothing I say or do will make a

61

difference. She has to want to change. Her addiction was dragging me down, and I couldn't let it anymore.

So I set hard limits.

Setting her and her problems aside, I finish my laundry and cleaning and eat my little frozen dinner chock full of sodium and regret.

I'm in bed by nine. You'd think a new girl in the city would be out partying on a Saturday night, but I need sleep more than I need air at this point.

Mr. Sandman is barely brushing soothing fingers over my brain when a noise wakes me up. A thump.

My eyes open to the dark room.

At least the lights are still off this time.

There's another thump from somewhere down the hall.

I take a deep breath. It's nothing. A neighbor.

Wait.

Something moved. A shadow. In my hall.

My *Supernatural* night-light is on, casting swirls of light and shade over the hall to the bathroom.

Somebody is there. I can just make out the outline of a person standing in the shadowed hall.

I can't move. What do I do? Race for my phone? But they might attack if they realize I'm awake. Would that scare them away or make it worse?

The dark figure shifts again, moving closer, nearly stepping into a ray of soft light cast from Dean's handsome face. The shadows against the wall shift and grow. But I can't make out any features. It's just a giant black blob.

More shuffling sounds.

I can't handle it anymore.

I scream.

The shadow races down the hall and I scramble for the phone on the bedside table, my fingers shaking so badly I can't even enter my code to unlock the screen.

62

A bang at the front door startles a shriek from my throat. Someone is out there, yelling.

"Bethany, are you okay?" the muffled voice says.

I fly to the door, pressing my face to the peephole.

Steven.

I unlock the two deadbolts, chain, and knob lock and pull the door open, stepping out and then shutting the door behind me. I'm not in the apartment. I'm safe.

"Someone's in there," I tell him, my voice shaking. "I can't call." I hold up my phone.

That's when I realize Steven isn't alone.

There's a girl with him.

"Are you okay?" she asks.

"Yes," I say, my voice shaking and unconvincing.

Steven pulls his phone out of the pocket of his pajama pants. They have birds all over them. Flamingos.

The woman with him is wearing bird pants, too, but hers are covered in crows.

What the hell? The total randomness of this entire situation pierces my shock and I have the sudden urge to burst into laughter.

"Let me call for you." As weird as this whole thing is, Steven's voice is calm and his presence is steadying as he talks to the 9-1-1 operator and tells them our location. He hands me the phone and I shakily try to explain what happened while Steven listens, his brows furrowed, a frown marring his normally happy, porn-stache face.

The operator keeps me on the line while the cops are en route, asking me questions about what happened.

In between everything, Steven introduces me to his bird friend. "Natalie Furmeyer," he tells me. It sounds familiar. I think he mentioned they had a new cult member. She's pretty, tall, and thin with long brown hair and a beaky nose, which is sort of ironic.

The cops arrive, a man and woman. The guy looks younger than me with a military haircut. He's only a few inches above my own five foot four. The woman is taller, maybe my age with a heart-shaped face and hair pulled back into a severe knot at the base of her neck.

They both have nametags over their right breast.

They search the apartment—it doesn't take long—and return with nothing but questions.

"It's empty," Officer K. Roberts says, his voice carefully neutral.

I rush inside and scan the hall, where I saw the figure. Nothing. They have the hall closet standing open, lights all on. Empty.

"Will you tell us everything that happened?" Officer J. Cutler asks, getting out her notepad and pen.

I repeat the story.

They don't look impressed. Or concerned at all.

So of course I make things so much better by spilling everything they don't need or want to know. Out comes all the weird things that have been happening over the last couple of months, the strange sounds, and the light coming on and the window being open in the middle of the night.

But the more I talk and try to explain, the less they believe me. I can tell by the look they exchange once they're finished writing out my statement.

"Ma'am, did you say you recently had some security tapes installed?" the younger guy asks.

I'm so not old enough to be a ma'am.

"Yes. It's connected to an app." Oh. Yeah, duh. I pull out my phone and we huddle around the screen. I pull up the video.

The only movement since I came up from the laundry earlier is when Steven and Natalie came over to bang on the door. We watch as I call the cops, and then the cops arrive.

"But I swear . . ."

Roberts is over by the window, his eyes scanning over the lock, which is engaged. "Are there any other ways to get inside this apartment?"

"Not that I know of." My face heats.

"Have you had anything to drink tonight?" Cutler asks.

"No," I say quickly.

They exchange another look and the guy shrugs. "There's not much more we can do, ma'am."

I nod. This is so embarrassing. "Thank you for your time, Officers."

They head to the door.

Steven puts a hand on my arm. "You can stay with—"

"Bethany?"

I spin at the sound of my name.

Brent is standing in the doorway.

Relief rolls over me. He's here. He came. He must have seen the commotion on the app.

He glances at the cops, then Steven and Natalie, and then back at me. With only a few long strides in my direction, he's right in front of me.

And because I haven't embarrassed myself enough for one evening, I fling myself into his arms, sticking to him like gum on a shoe.

"Is everything okay?" His hands rub my back, soothing me like I'm a cat and he's . . . catnip.

Really, it's the only explanation. And he does smell amazing, like cinnamon and man with a hint of expensive cologne.

"It's fine." I'm seriously burying myself in his chest. I could stay here forever. From far away, I hear the cops leaving, the static of their radios disappearing down the hall before I manage to pull myself away from Mr. Catnip.

Steven is still standing there a bit awkwardly which is like his MO anyway, and Natalie is next to him, shifting from one foot to another, her eyes not meeting anyone else's.

I tell Brent what happened, and how the cops couldn't find anything.

"They thought I was crazy. Or on drugs." I sigh and shake my head.

"Let me take a quick look, too." He squeezes my hand once, then gives Steven a quick nod before he takes a look around. He doesn't go far. There's not much to look at. The small hallway leads to the even smaller bathroom.

The light clicks on down the hall.

Steven clears his throat. "Call me if you need anything."

"Steven." I give him a hug. I have to. Then Natalie, too. "Thank you both for staying with me and helping me tonight. I really appreciate it."

With a small smile and a wave, they leave.

Then Brent's back. "I couldn't find anything. Pack a big bag. You're with me for the foreseeable future."

I should argue, but there's no way in hell I'm sleeping here tonight, so I follow directions with a nod, grateful to be leaving.

But then, as Brent's turning his fancy car onto East Fourteenth Street past tightly packed brick buildings and shops all dark and closed for the night, the doubts creep in. He can't really want me to stay with him, despite all of our friend talk and everything he's done and how nice he is. I mean, look at him. And look at me. I peer through the passenger window to the side mirror. My curly hair is utter chaos, poking in all sorts of directions. I have grey smudges under my eyes and pale, pasty skin. I look like a reincarnated dishrag.

"Are you sure you're okay with me staying with you?"

He glances over at me and then back at the road. "Of course."

Is he just saying that? I bite my lip. "I'm just not sure it's a good idea, long-term."

"Why not?"

"Because you're . . ." I wave my hand at him.

"What?" He's frowning.

I'm offending him. I have to tell him the truth. My nose wrinkles. "You're too good-looking."

"You really think so?" A slow grin spreads across his face.

"Don't act like you don't know it."

"Maybe I don't." He preens, batting his lashes at me and flicking fake hair over his shoulder. "Did you see that interesting building over there?" He points, stretching his arm in front of my face and flexing his bicep with exaggerated motions.

I swat his sexy arm away.

He laughs and pulls his muscles away from my face. "I promise I won't walk around in only a towel to tempt you."

"Gee, thanks. You think you're funny."

"I am funny. Why does it matter what I look like?"

"It doesn't matter. It's just that I don't want to cramp your style. You know, if you're going to be having lady friends over, or whatever." I hold my breath.

His reaction is a surprised blink and lifting of his eyebrows. "Oh. Lady friends."

He's silent for way too long. "See? It's a bad idea, right?"

"No, that's not it. It's just, with the season starting and Dad wanting me to spend time with his investors, plus the charity work . . . I've got too much to do. I haven't had time lately for . . . lady friends."

Oh boy, this is awkward. He doesn't have a new skank over every night? That can't be true. He's the hottest man in the damn world. And rich. And famous. Guys like him don't have empty beds.

"You told me, and I quote, 'I get plenty of hanky-panky.'"

"I do. Just not right now." He glances over at me. "Unless you're bringing this up because you're trying to be polite and the truth is you don't want *me* cramping *your* style because you want to have male . . . you know, companions, or whatever."

"Oh, no." I laugh. "No, no, no. I'm off that train." I bite my lip and say in a lower voice. "Except for Tuesday. That's orgy night."

He chokes.

"I'm kidding!"

Then he's laughing and coughing. "I just choked on my own spit."

I nod solemnly. "I have that effect on people."

Chapter Nine

Girls like Zac Efron and true crime.
–Karen Kilgariff
My Favorite Murder episode 69

Brent

"I'm going to pretend I'm not offended you still haven't called me to make sure I'm still alive after snowboarding again for the first time in nearly twenty years. I'll save you the suspense. Yes, I'm still alive. No, I'm not calling you from beyond the grave."

The line hums in silence for a few seconds and then he speaks in a lower voice. *"It was weird though. Being at the top of the mountain. Just before we went down, I was scared. Terrified out of my mind, actually. But then I got this feeling, like Mom was there, telling me it was going to be okay. I could even smell her, that sweet lemon scent she always wore."* He sighs. *"You think I've lost it, right? Anyway. We're heading to Pakistan tomorrow and I probably won't be able to call or email again for a while. I hope you're doing okay."*

I am doing okay. But I still don't call Marc back.

A couple of days pass as I settle into my new, odd, sort-of companionable living situation. It's kind of nice. And what I told Bethany in the car turns out to be true. We don't see each other much.

It's a double-edged sword. Part of me wants to see her, but then another part of me is grateful for the reprieve. I'm happy to be helping her, but I can't get too close to anyone right now. Especially someone as enticing as she is.

She's a considerate roomie. She always puts the toothpaste cap back on, changes the toilet paper roll, and sets up the coffee when she leaves before me.

In exchange, I've been cooking extra during my meal prep and leaving her plates of food in the fridge to reheat when she gets home. It's leftovers of what I eat, so mostly healthy, but she seems to enjoy it since it disappears promptly.

Today I had the MRI and it was terrible. Trapped inside a humming tube for two hours is not the best way to spend my time. And now I'm exhausted. I won't get the results for another week and then I know Dr. Richards will pressure me to discuss options with a cardiovascular surgeon. I'm going to have to make a real choice. But every choice takes me to the same inevitable conclusion. Surgery. An end to everything I've worked for my entire life.

To drag myself out of the funk, I order food I never allow myself to eat from my favorite Chinese takeout place. Eating and watching my favorite show will help. Maybe.

Bethany usually works late during the week, so I have the place to myself, for now.

I'm on the couch in my sweats, takeout all around me, when the door opens and heels tap in the entryway. There's a noisy inhale and then she groans. "Something smells delicious. Did you cook . . . ?"

I twist my head around from my position on the couch and find her standing at the threshold to the living room, mouth open, eyes on the TV.

"Oh my God, are you watching *Forensic Files*?" She flicks her shoes off into the corner, her purse drops on a side table, and then she's next to me on the couch, eyes still trained on the TV. "Oh, I've seen this one. The husband did it."

"Hey." I nudge her with a knee. "Spoiler alert."

"Sorry. Can I have some of this?" She points at the plethora of half-full containers I've left on the coffee table. "Is that chow mein?" She picks up a carton and the fork I left on the table and digs in before I have a chance to nod in assent.

I watch her, amused.

"Have you seen the one where the senator hit the pedestrian? That one is my favorite. Fucking politicians."

"Your favorite . . . what, your favorite murder?"

"For this show I guess. I have other ones. Yes, I know it's weird, but I have a true-crime thing. I just love it." She stops and grimaces at me. "Are you going to kick me out now? I promise I won't murder you."

"Well, if you *promise* you won't murder me, then I guess it's okay. I get it. I have a murder thing, too." I gesture at the TV. "Obviously."

"You do? Damn. That's going to make it harder to explain the lime delivery I have coming in next week."

I laugh. "What's coming next? Clown makeup?"

She gasps. "This is amazing. No one ever gets my John Wayne Gacy jokes."

I tsk. "Sounds like your friends are a bunch of losers who don't understand serial-killer humor. So what got you into true crime?"

She chews her food and considers the question before responding. "There's a lot of reasons. I don't know. I guess I always just find it sort of fascinating. Like why do people think that way? Who has a problem with someone and jumps to murder as the solution? It's nuts. Plus it's a safe way to prepare myself for if I'm ever in a situation where I might be murdered. It alleviates all my 'maybe I'm going to die today' anxieties. It's probably hard to imagine since you're such a beefcake, but there's always some anxiety involved in being a woman. You can't even walk by a stranger on a street in broad daylight without wondering if they're going to attack you."

"That makes sense. And despite the beefcake appearance," I roll my eyes and nudge her with my shoulder, "I do sort of know what you mean. I've had a few stalkers. And I had a woman try to kill me. It does make one a bit jumpy."

She gasps. "That's right! I saw it on the news and I guess I just didn't think about it because you're . . . well, you, but oh my God. You were almost murdered." She leans forward. "Tell me *everything*." Her hand is back on my arm and her eyes are riveted on mine.

Her excitement is contagious. A spark of energy clicks to life inside me. "There's not much to tell. Marissa was a reporter for *Stylz*. She dated Marc for a short time. He broke up with her when he walked in on her propositioning me. Naked."

She grimaces. "Sounds like a bad soap opera."

I laugh. "It felt like a bad soap opera. After her plan to seduce me didn't work, she wrote an article accusing me of sexual assault."

"That's why you and Gwen did the whole fake-dating thing."

I sigh and roll my eyes. "Yes. That was a dumb decision. At least it brought Marc and Gwen together. But anyway, what I didn't know at the time was that Marissa had not only used Marc to get to me, she had also been sending me anonymous letters and weird, creepy fan mail. I get a lot of threats and strange women having delusions that we're in a serious relationship, but I never thought they would come from someone I knew

72

personally. Even someone as crazy as Marissa. After she ran a horrible article about Gwen and Marc, I had my attorney sue her for defamation, and well, she didn't take it kindly."

"That was the article that outed Gwen and Marc's relationship, right?"

"Right."

"While you were fake-dating her."

"Yes."

"But didn't you like Gwen, too?"

"I did. And I was upset at the time, but then I realized what Marc felt for Gwen was different. For me, she was a nice, normal woman I thought I could develop something with. Marc loved her."

She snorts. "Nice normal supermodel."

"Yeah, but you know Gwen. She's chill."

"She is. Super nice. Can't hate her. Dammit."

I grin. "It all worked out."

"Except you got shot."

"Right, well, after Marissa got notice of the lawsuit, she showed up at my apartment, yelling and screaming. Some paper and pictures fell out of her purse and that's when I realized she was my stalker."

"Ho-ly shit." She puts the chow mein container back on the table and tucks her legs under her on the couch next to me.

My eyes are drawn to her sleek legs and tiny toes. She's so delicate and small, it brings out some kind of protective instinct in me. I want to throw her over my shoulder like a caveman and drag her off somewhere.

Which sounds awful. And since humankind has progressed somewhat since the Neolithic period, perhaps I should amend that statement to add I want to drag her off with her enthusiastic consent and treat her with the utmost respect.

I clear my throat. "When I called her out for being the stalker and threatened to file charges and a restraining order, she pulled out a gun and shot me. Here." I pull the sleeve of my shirt up to show her the scar on my arm.

She traces the small mark with a finger. "Wow." Her breath puffs against my shoulder and a thrill of awareness shoots down from the small touch on my arm to my stomach. All too soon she pulls back. "What happened to Marissa?"

I clear my throat and focus on her question. "She was charged with second-degree attempted murder because they couldn't prove it was premeditated."

"Uh, I think showing up to your place with a gun is pretty premeditated."

"You'd think so. But she also had a psychologist testify she wasn't of sound mind, and while they couldn't prove insanity, the court was pretty lenient since it's her first offense and they think she could improve with proper treatment. She got five years, but she could be released sooner with good behavior."

Bethany shakes her head. "Unbelievable. I fucking hate that. They're always giving attempted murderers a break, and why? Because the person they tried to kill had the audacity to survive? It makes me real punchy."

I laugh. "Tell me about it. I've always been into true crime, but after all that happened, it made me even more curious to try and understand why people do the things they do."

"My friend Ted thinks my true-crime obsession is why I'm overreacting to all the strangeness in the apartment."

"I don't know. I think you should always trust your instincts. It's better to be overly cautious and wrong than not cautious enough and dead."

"That's very true. Death would be bad. But I don't think whatever's going on in my apartment is going to lead to my imminent demise. There's probably a plausible explanation. And it is possible I imagined the whole figure-in-the-shadows thing. It might have been pareidolia."

"Para-what?"

"I'm probably saying it wrong. My friend Lucy sent me an article about it the other day. It's when your brain incorrectly interprets shadows and lights into a recognizable form—it's why kids see a figure in their closet when it's actually a coat or something." She sighs. "And I feel really bad for taking up space in your apartment. You can't enjoy me being here, eating your food, spoiling your shows . . ."

"I like having you here. I'm used to having someone around since I've been living with Marc. It sucks to be alone."

She bites her lip. "What about Angela?"

"Who?"

Her brows lift. "Angela Sinclair? Isn't she your . . ." A hand waves in my direction, toward my lap. "You know."

I laugh. "My *you know*? No, I don't know."

She clucks in frustration. "The gossip columns say you guys are an item. But I haven't seen her over here. I'm in the way, aren't I?"

"Okay, hold up. First off, I told you before, I don't have time for lady friends, remember? Second, gossip columns are ninety-nine percent bullshit. I barely know Angela. Our fathers are doing business together and I've met her twice. And okay, Dad has actually thrown me in her direction numerous times, despite my best efforts. I wouldn't be surprised if he informed the paparazzi of that bullshit himself. He's trying to hook us up because he wants our families to combine empires." I roll my eyes. "But it's not happening."

"So you didn't go over to Angela's apartment last week for a little . . . hanky-panky?"

I chuckle. "No. Angela's nice, but she's not my type." I'm surprised she even knows I went over there. It was the same night I brought her the security stuff. A light clicks on. "Is that what you thought? That I went over to Angela's for . . . relations and then went to your place with the pizza? And then I was going back there when I left? Is that why you were so weird?"

"I wasn't weird." The words come out too quickly, running together.

"Yes, you were. You told me to drive carefully so I didn't end up in a sinkhole."

"Okay, I was weird." She grimaces. "I'm sorry. It's really none of my business what you do in your, ah, spare time."

I smile. I kinda like that she cares. "I'm using my spare time to help you figure out what's happening in your apartment. Not because I want to get rid of you, but because I want to make sure you don't get murdered. Is there anyone who wants to hurt you that you know of?"

"I literally know two people in the city." She fiddles with the edge of her skirt, as if embarrassed to admit this little nugget of info. "And you're one of them."

"Who's the other one?"

She grins. "Your dad. He's a pig, but I don't think he's a murderer."

"Yeah, he needs you too much to put out a hit."

"Thankfully. So, what do we do about my apartment? How are we going to solve this mystery, Scoob?"

"Hmm." I rub my chin. "Let's see the spreadsheet again."

She unfolds herself from the couch and grabs her laptop from the bag she left by the door before resuming her spot next to me.

It takes a couple minutes for her to power up the computer.

Once it's up, I glance over the data. "This is really impressively color coded."

"I'm a great secretary. I know it's weird, but I am *good* at it. Not exactly what most people want to do with their lives, but I'm good at anticipating needs and tackling details. Managing stuff, tracking data, and analyzing reports." She shrugs. "And I love doing it."

"There's nothing wrong with that."

She scoffs. "Says the second-round draft pick."

A rush of pride surprises me. I didn't know she knew anything about me, she always seems so unimpressed. "You been reading up on me?"

She shrugs. "I like football."

"Who's your team?"

"Oakland."

I groan. "That's it. We can't be friends."

She punches me in the arm. "Don't be such an East Coast West Coast rapper."

"I'll try, but this might be a deal breaker."

She rolls her eyes but then smiles at me. "Anyway, Friday seems likely for some action. Or it has been three out of the last four weekends."

"And you've never tried to locate the source on your own?"

"What? No way. That's like one of the basic laws of not getting murdered. Stay out of the forest, don't pick up hitchhikers—even if they have a broken arm—and don't investigate strange noises. All of that leads to murder."

"Good point. So Friday night we can hang at your place and wait for the weirdness to begin. If anything happens, we can search together."

She bites her lip. "Are you sure?"

"Yes. I wouldn't offer if I really didn't want to help. Besides, someone got in your apartment and it wasn't through the door."

"Thank you for believing me. You have to let me repay you somehow. Seriously. I am in your debt for reals. I don't have money but I'm great at making color-coded lists and organizing chaos." She nudges me with a shoulder.

I consider her bright eyes and an idea flashes through me. "Actually, you might be able to help me with something. And it wouldn't cost more than your time."

"Anything."

"How are you at event planning?"

~*~

"Are you here to see Bethany?"

The man holding the door open for me is familiar. I recognize the meticulously groomed yet amazingly thick mustache. It's Bethany's neighbor. The one who helped her when the cops were called.

"Yeah. Thanks, man." I nod in recognition. "Steven, right?"

He nods. He's on his way out and he's not alone. I recognize the diminutive brunette next to him. We didn't get a chance to meet the other night.

"This is my girlfriend. Natalie Furmeyer."

78

"Nice to meet you," I say.

"We're going birding," Steven continues.

Natalie smiles at me, the gesture small and polite, and then she looks down at her feet.

Maybe she recognizes me? People generally respond one of two ways when we meet. They're either overly exuberant and all over me or they're shocked into silence and running away. Kind of like my romantic relationships.

I step back toward the elevator and hit the button. "That's great."

"We met through the ornithology club," Steven continues. "We just came up with a name for the club the other night. We've decided to call it Frequent Flyers. Get it? Flyer?"

They're wearing matching polo shirts, and they each have binoculars around their necks.

"That's . . ." I probably shouldn't say great again. "Cool. You guys have a good night."

The elevator dings.

Saved by the bell.

Steven is still standing there, watching me as the doors slide shut.

Weird. I don't remember him being so odd before. Then again, I wasn't paying attention to him. I was more concerned with Bethany.

It's Friday night and Bethany insisted on providing dinner at her place while we have our little stakeout. Since I've been cooking for us so much, the massive amounts of guilt are eating her alive. Her words. She also said if I didn't let her feed me, she'd paint giant octopus testicles on my face while I slept. I chuckle. She always says the craziest things.

We've also gotten in the habit of leaving each other random, silly notes. Yesterday's were my favorite.

Thank you for always feeding me. I can already feel the vegan powers developing. B

You're welcome. The trash is going out today, so if you have to dispose of any bodies, now's the time. B

Dammit I have to change my killing schedule to next week! B

She answers the door in yoga pants and a T-shirt, her hair pulled back in a messy knot. They're the simple clothes she typically wears when she's not working, but there's something about seeing the slope of her neck and the curve of her ear that makes my stomach somersault and my heart hammer.

"You didn't need me to buzz you in." Her lips purse. "Is the building door broken again?"

I frown. "Again?"

She waves me off and then claps. "I got burgers and murders!"

I follow her into the living room.

She has the food plated on the coffee table and the TV is set to the most recent true-crime documentary to hit streaming services.

"You really know how to show a guy a good time." I take off my jacket and sling it over the chair.

"I know, right? We gotta have something to keep us occupied while we wait for the weird."

"Thank you for getting the food, but seriously, does the building door break a lot?"

"Sometimes the lock is jiggly." She purses her lips. "Kind of like my ass."

I laugh but then cut it off quick. Wait. That's not good. My lips tug down as I sit beside her on the small futon. "I don't think it's broken now. Steven let me in. He was heading out to bird-watch with his girlfriend."

80

"Ah yes, Natalie Furmeyer, fellow bird lover."

"Yeah. They seem . . . interesting."

She laughs and gives me a look like she knows exactly what I'm thinking. "It's the mustache. It threw me off at first, too. Don't worry, he's harmless except for the never-ending conversations about birds."

We dig into our burgers. "They came up with their club name. Did you know?" I ask after swallowing my first bite.

Her eyes widen. "They did? What is it?"

"Frequent Flyers."

"Oh my. That's punny."

"It sure is."

"It makes sense now."

"What does?"

"Why Steven is so hawkward." She nudges me with her elbow. "Get it? Hawk-ward?"

I groan. "Oh, no."

"I quack you up, right?" She slaps her leg and laughs so hard at her own terrible joke I can't help but join in.

I nudge her with a shoulder. "Toucan play at that game."

She gasps and cracks up. "Yes! No harm no fowl."

"If you have more, I'm owl ears."

She falls against me, laughing.

"Those were the lamest jokes I've ever made," I say, but I'm wiping tears from my eyes.

I haven't laughed this hard in a long time. My cheeks hurt from the strain.

We spend the next hour eating our burgers and watching the show she put on, guessing about whether the person is innocent or not. The conversation is easy and flowing and full of humor.

When the food is done, I help her clean up and we go back to the couch.

Halfway through season two, she yawns.

A few minutes later, her eyes are blinking to stay open.

And then not long after that, she's out. Her mouth hangs ajar and she's breathing softly while her honey-colored curls reach for me across the back of the couch.

It's kind of cute, actually.

I shut the TV off and most of the lights, leaving just the hall light on. Then I cover her with the blanket from the back of the couch. She murmurs and rolls in my direction, her head landing on my shoulder.

It's quiet in the dim room and my eyes get heavy, but the feel of Bethany's curves pressed to my side keeps me awake. As far as my health conditions go, I have more pressing issues than a limp dick. But when an attractive woman is pressed against me—one I actually like—it's hard not to think about.

Hard being the operative word.

A state I have not been able to achieve in months.

But the lack of an erection doesn't stop my heart from pounding at her tempting closeness, at her soft breath hitting my neck, or her full breast pressed into my side.

I take a slow, deep pull of air into my lungs and then release it, trying to relax.

Eventually, the sounds of even breathing and distant traffic lull me into a light sleep. Until a warm hand lands on my stomach.

I jolt awake.

"Do you hear that?" she whispers.

It takes me a few seconds to focus. My entire being is fixated on the location of her hand. It's on my stomach, lower stomach. Close to . . . another area.

I shove those thoughts away. I can barely hear it, a kind of rhythmic knocking.

She moves away, taking the heat with her, leaving a cold reminder behind.

I follow. The sounds are coming from somewhere above the hall closet.

"Where does this lead?" I ask in a low voice.

"How am I supposed to know? I've never crawled around in any ventilation."

"Maybe we should try and get a copy of the building plans."

The sound cuts off suddenly.

I open the closet door and poke around. It's a shallow, narrow space with sweaters and a couple of coats hanging up. I push the coats aside until I find the back wall. There's nothing else in here. No vents or cracks in the plaster or anything out of the ordinary.

"Maybe it's from a TV or something in another apartment?" I suggest.

"What kind of TV show is just a bunch of knocking and banging?"

I shrug. "People are weird. Let's see if we can hear it from the floor above. Or anywhere else on this floor."

Time to investigate the strange noise.

We lock the front door and then head down the hallway, stopping to listen periodically.

Nothing. Steven and Martha's place is quiet. The Frequent Flyers must have left for the night.

We head to the stairwell.

On the floor above, we walk down the hall together, stopping at intervals to listen carefully.

She stops, grabbing my arm. "Did you hear that?"

"No."

We sit in silence for a minute. Then I hear it. A knocking and then a low moan.

"I think it's coming from this way." I walk in the direction of the sound to the nearest apartment and lean against the door. There's another weird, garbled yell and then a muffled shout.

I get closer, pressing my ear closer to the hard wood.

"There's something really—" My words cut off as the door swings open and I fall inside.

Chapter Ten

Adversity is an opportunity for heroism.
–Mark Levy

Bethany

I watch Brent disappear into the doorway and my heart drops with his fall.

"Brent!" I rush toward him and then stop in my tracks.

There's a middle-aged man standing at the door. He has a receding hairline, thick black-rimmed glasses, and a scrawny white chest covered in dark hair. The only thing he's wearing is some kind of oddly fashioned underwear. I can't help but stare down at it.

It's a thong shaped like a pink elephant with the trunk covering his crotch.

Once I've taken all that in, I glance up into the apartment. There are people in all stages of undress behind him. At least a dozen men and women. Tall and short and thin and naked and middle aged to old and wow this is quite the . . . orgy.

Oh. My. God.

"Are you here for the party? I really hope so," pink elephant man says.

Brent's still on his knees from his inglorious fall. He hasn't moved. Maybe the shock of being eye level with elephant-covered junk has incapacitated him.

"Do you guys have these, uh, parties often?" I ask.

"You two interested in joining us?" He winks at Brent.

Brent wakes from his frozen terror and leaps to his feet, eyes wide, face red. He puts a hand on the small of my back to guide me away from the scene.

But I can't leave yet. "Do you guys do this every week?" I call out over my shoulder.

"Just once a month, sugar, second Friday! If you can convince your man, I'll be here waiting." He sings the words.

I'm disappointed in his answer—wild orgies apparently aren't the answer to the strange knocking sounds—and Brent's hand on my back is pushing me so urgently now I'm really struggling not to laugh.

"We won't be back," Brent calls. "We're at the wrong door."

"It might be the right door, sugar!" pink elephant yells as we're turning the corner back to the stairs.

I completely lose it. I'm laughing so hard, tears are running down my face. "I . . . can't . . . believe . . . that was a real orgy."

"And it's not even Tuesday," Brent deadpans.

Now we're both laughing hard.

"Did you see his face?" I wipe the tears from my eyes. "He was super into you."

"Yeah, I'm thinking we should call it a night with that one."

"But who knows what else is going on around here? Is that what the sound has been this whole time? People knocking . . . boots?"

"It would be weird if everyone in this building waited to have sex until Gwen moved out."

"Good point."

Back in the apartment, there's no more knocking sounds. All is silent and mostly dark. Only the hall light is still on. We resume our positions on the futon.

"Do you think there will be any more noises tonight?" Brent asks.

"I'm not sure. I don't usually stick around after the initial burst."

"We can get more data for your spreadsheet."

"Oh lovely, lovely spreadsheets," I sigh.

He chuckles. "Did your obsession start as a child or is this a recent fascination?"

"I've always loved analyzing data."

"And that's what led you to your job working for the biggest asshole in New York City?"

His tone is dry, but his words strike a chord in my chest that I recognize all too well. I know what it's like to swallow a bitter taste in your mouth every time you talk about a parent. "Your dad isn't really an asshole. He's just kind of old-school."

"That's one way to put it. An incredibly kind, sugar-coated way."

"What can I say? I'm just one of those full of love kind of people." I wink. "Seriously though, I'm super grateful Marc gave me this opportunity. I was so ready for a change and to get away from—" *My mother.* "Everything."

"Running away from something?"

"Escaping, more like it."

"Bad relationship?"

Part of me wants to tell him everything. He would understand, since he has parental troubles as well. Another part of me is so used to holding back, I can't help but avoid exposing too much.

"You could say that," I hedge. "My mom is a bit of a level ten clinger. It was time to cut the cord." And it's

87

also time for a subject change. "But really, Marc is great. You're so lucky to have him as a brother."

"Very true. You have any siblings?"

"Nope. Only child. I've always wished I did have brothers or sisters." Someone to share the responsibility of Mom with.

"I don't know what I would have done without Marc after our mom died."

I bite my lip. "I'm sorry."

He shrugs off my condolences. "It was a long time ago."

"My dad died when I was young, too."

His eyes focus on mine. "What happened?"

"Unintentional poisoning." I used the nice, clinical term for an overdose. No need to get into all that. "It's part of the reason my mom is so needy."

A crease forms between his brows. "What—?"

"How old were you when your mom passed?"

He blinks at the subject change, but doesn't push it. "Ten. Marc was fourteen. She—" He cuts off and rubs his forehead before continuing. "She had a heart condition. We didn't know. Dad was . . . Well, he didn't take it well, to put it lightly. It was really unexpected and he just sort of disappeared. He was always busy with work, but Mom was the one person who could pull him from it. Once she was gone, he lost himself even more to the company. Marc became a surrogate parent. Always taking care of me." He sighs. "I'm glad he's out there, enjoying his life." He smiles, but the gesture doesn't reach his eyes.

Simple jealousy that his brother got the girl? Or is it something more complex? "So did he go snowboarding yet?"

This time the smile is one hundred percent real. "Oh yeah. Kicked butt doing it, too. I wish I could have been there with him. I didn't think I would miss him this much. But it's been weird since he's been gone. Lonely, almost."

"Huh. I guess I never thought about hot, rich, and famous people as being lonely."

He grins. "You think I'm hot, huh?"

I roll my eyes. "Don't let your ego take up all the space in here."

He laughs softly. "It's not ego. Trust me."

We're silent then for a few long minutes, but it's not uncomfortable. The sounds of distant traffic are soothing and with the lights down, I almost start to nod off until Brent shifts next to me.

"Let's pull the bed out," he says in a low voice. "You're falling asleep on me."

I smile and get up to help him lay the futon flat and grab the comforter from underneath.

We lie down, facing each other in the dim light.

"This is weird." I yawn.

"You've said that before." His voice is low and warm in the dark, like a rich chocolate.

"We have a lot of awkward moments together. It's like our thing. You know, some people are like, we always meet at happy hour, or I always see you at the gym. But us? We have the market cornered on weird. How many other friends have you staked out apartments with, looking for ghosts?"

"You are definitely the first. Does being here on your bed together make it uncomfortable? I can sit on the chair or on the floor."

"No. Oddly, it doesn't. I like our creepy interludes."

"I like them, too."

Silence descends, and in the quiet, I can't help but think Brent isn't a man-ho or a douche-nugget or like I would have thought a famous, rich, successful football player would be. He's kind. Considerate. Sensitive. He's not a frog, he's a prince.

I fall asleep to the steady sounds of his breathing.

Although we fall into dreamland apart, we wake up together, wrapped in a cocoon of warmth. Brent is once again the big spoon.

His breath puffs steadily in my ear.

His arms are wrapped around me from behind like he can't get close enough. I have front-row seating to his strong, tan forearms. I could lie here forever.

I wiggle a little and something important dawns on me.

He's not hard.

At all.

Aaand this explains why we're just friends.

He can't be my Prince Charming because he's not attracted to me, obviously. Although I always thought morning wood was an involuntary thing, like a guy could have a three-legged puke-green troll with a giant nose and red eyes in his armpits and still wake up with a boner.

Am I so unappealing? No wonder I'm the only single chick left standing in my group of friends. No one told me, I'm disgusting.

His breathing changes, drawing in on a sharp intake and then he pulls away quickly, taking his heat with him.

I stay still and keep my breathing even, not wanting him to know I'm awake.

Of course he wouldn't want me. He wants girls like Gwen and Angela Sinclair, former models and rich people who belong in his world. I'm just . . . me. Normal. Boring. Blah.

I wait until he heads for the bathroom, and then I get out of bed, grabbing my night robe and wrapping it around myself like a shield.

Friends. We are just friends.

By the time Brent exits the bathroom, I have coffee brewing and a selection of cheap, generic cereal on the counter. I've also gathered all my insecurities and forged them into my armor of humor. It's what I do best.

"Fruity Os or Captain Not-So-Crunchy?" I shake the box at him. "I was going to cook you some Belgian waffles and gourmet omelets but I didn't want to wow you too much with my prowess in the kitchen because then you'd fall in love with me and I'd have to leave you eventually for Chris Evans."

He chuckles. "Really? Set aside like so much trash for Captain America?"

I shrug. "Sorry. He's my boo."

He grabs the box of cereal from my hand and shakes some into a bowl.

"So last night was a bust." He pours milk into the bowl and then shoves a bite into his mouth.

"A bust, a cock, some saggy boobs, a bit of hairy man chest."

He chokes.

"Last night was a lot of things," I add.

"You need to stop making me choke. I think you really are trying to kill me."

"I would never. But I did have an idea. You mentioned getting plans for the building last night, and I think it's a good idea. My friend Sam is an architect. I'm going to call him for help."

"Sam?"

Is that a twinge of jealousy I hear in the voice of Mr. I Have No Morning Wood? Not likely. Just wishful thinking.

"Yeah. He's Gemma's boyfriend. Gwen's sister."

"Right."

We finish up our breakfasts and drink our coffee in comfortable silence. It feels like we've done this a hundred times when he takes my bowl and proceeds to wash it for me and place it on the drying rack. It feels even more natural when we chat about our plans for the day, and he asks me to meet up later for dinner at his apartment.

And it only stings a little bit when I force myself to tell him I have work and laundry to do, so I will be back at his place super late.

And when he hugs me goodbye, it's the most normal thing in the world to try to hold on to the feeling of warmth and safety for as long as possible because I know that while I'm starting to feel things for him, he doesn't feel the same.

I have to pull away. I have to stop staring at his biceps and eyes and perfectly chiseled jawline like I want to worship him with my tongue.

I can't hang out with him like we have been, laughing and joking while he offers me glimpses of all his most vulnerable pieces. He's chipping away at the walls I've built around my heart, the emotions I'm saving for someone who will stick around.

Someone who actually wants me back.

Chapter Eleven

Do you know what my favorite part of the game is? The opportunity to play.
–Mike Singletary

Brent

"Don't stick your elbows out. You'll strain your shoulder joints." I tap Rodrigues on the arm and he pulls his elbows in.

I'm well aware of the irony here, helping a teammate avoid injury when I shouldn't even be working out.

He finishes his reps and rolls to a stand. "Thanks for spotting me, man. And for the tips. Those grip drills really helped."

"Anytime. I saw you on the field yesterday. You caught at least twice as many jump balls."

We bump fists and then he wanders off to some other rookies hanging around the squat rack.

Satisfaction sings through me. Helping someone else succeed is almost as fulfilling as achieving it myself.

My phone chirps. It's Roger.

"We got an offer from the Sharks."

"What is it?"

"Six years, fifty-four million. I negotiated a signing bonus and over a million in potential incentives. We can go over it together tomorrow morning before you sign."

"Right."

My heart thumps in my chest. I have a doctor's appointment tomorrow morning to go over the results of the MRI.

This should be fantastic news, but I can't muster the enthusiasm I know Roger expects.

"I'm . . . in shock, I think." I force out a laugh. "How about tomorrow afternoon?"

The clock is ticking. I can't sign this contract in good faith. Not without coming clean. It's not fair to the team. Right? But how could I just leave football?

"That's great, Brent. I can see you at three."

We hang up and I head to the locker room, rubbing my chest, trying to soothe the building anxiety.

What is Roger going to think? Dad is going to freak. I'm going to lose this contract. End my career. Dad's company . . . they won't want me as the face of the business when I'm no longer a sports superstar.

I wish I could talk to someone.

Bethany.

I haven't seen her much lately. Granted, I've been busy helping with training, and she's been helping the kids club organize the charity baseball game. Plus she's got her job and I have my dealings with Dad and doctors.

Maybe I'm being paranoid, but I think she's avoiding me.

I texted her this morning to see if she'd heard anything back from her architect friend, but she still hasn't responded.

The other night at her apartment was . . . fun. Weird, all things and pink elephants considered, but nice.

She listened to my sob stories without judgment or pity. It's like she actually cares about me and not what I have to offer. Which, frankly, isn't much at the moment.

After showering, I head to the Bronx. I've been meaning to stop by to see if there's anything else I can do to help with the charity event, and also to see how Bethany has been progressing.

The front office is bustling with activity. Normally, there are only a few people there, including the director, Rosemarie, but right now there are about a half dozen people sorting envelopes, working on computers, and making copies as I walk in. I recognize more than one face.

My eyes snag on one in particular.

What is Angela Sinclair doing here? Did my father—?

"Brent," Bethany calls. She's in the back corner, leaning over someone at a computer screen. The redhead sitting next to her is a welcome face. Charlie.

"Hey." I weave through a few desks to reach her. "I see you've gotten some recruits."

Bethany grins.

"Hey, Charlie." I meant to contact her myself, but Bethany obviously beat me to it. When she's not working for my father in IT, Charlie helps maintain the website for the kids club. As a good friend of Marc's, of course she'd be here to help out in a pinch.

"Yeah, I needed someone to hack into June's computer since no one can reach her for the password," Bethany says. "Rosemarie has a list of people who've volunteered before and I recognized Charlie's name."

"And, um," I tilt my head in Angela's direction, "where did you find these other volunteers?"

Her smile is devilish. "Mr. Crawford was surprisingly forthcoming with certain people's contact information when I told him I needed help for your charity game."

"Uh-huh, I bet he was." My eyes narrow but before I can question her further on why she would be helping Dad with his schemes, Angela is standing next to me.

"Hey, Brent," she coos. She's wearing a white polo shirt and cream pants with a sharp crease running down each leg. Her hair is pulled back into a harsh French twist, not a hair out of place. "Bethany, I finished with the mailers. Is there anything else I can help with?"

"How are you with computers?"

She shrugs. "I've got some experience."

"Great. Will you help Charlie? I have something to show Brent."

Angela nods as Bethany takes my arm and pulls me to the other side of the room.

"What are you up to?" I ask.

We sit down next to each other at one of the desks. Her laptop rests on one side and an organizer stuffed with colorful bits of paper sits next to it.

"Me?" Her eyes are wide and innocent. Unlike Angela, Bethany's hair is falling around her shoulders in furious waves. Strands fly around her face and down her neck, enticing the eye to follow. She's wearing her normal, professional office attire, but there's a coffee stain on her white sleeve.

"Why is . . ." I glance over at Angela and Charlie. They're focused on the computer and not paying attention to us. Still. I lower my voice. "Angela Sinclair here?"

She shrugs. "I needed more bodies. She's actually been really helpful. Look, Brent, I'm not in on your dad's whole conspiracy. I didn't even know you would be here, but I'm glad you came. Charlie hacked into June's computer and it was worse than we thought. She barely has any sponsors lined up and now we have less than two weeks, but I had an idea."

"Shoot."

She bites her lip. The twinkle in her eyes makes her look like a devious pixie, the kind who lures unsuspecting men into the fairy world. "I was thinking about making a calendar featuring you and some guys from the team."

My brows lift. "Okay."

"Topless."

I laugh.

"And holding puppies."

"Puppies?"

"Or kittens. Maybe a bunny for April."

"Um. Isn't that exactly what you didn't want me to do?"

"Exactly! Women—and men—will die to have topless pictures of sexy football men holding baby animals. I'm telling you." Her eyes brighten with excitement. "We can tease it prior to the game and then sell the actual calendars at the event, exclusively. Plus, normally they have sponsor posters on the field and ads in the schedule, but this way we can put adverts in the calendar that people can look at all year long. It might entice some people to buy ad space."

I smile at her. "Of course I'm in. It's a great idea. You need me to recruit some guys from the team?"

She nods and gives me a relieved smile. "Thank you so much. I know you've been super busy and I hate to take up more of your time, but I swear it will be quick. I already have a photographer lined up and she can go to the players on their schedule so it won't be an inconvenience."

"It's no problem. You're doing so much to help the kids club. I really appreciate it."

She eyes me carefully, her gaze running over my face. "Are you sure? You've been working a lot. You look tired."

I scratch the back of my head and squint at the floor. "It's always exhausting when training starts."

Even though it hasn't really ramped up yet. Normally, I would be fine. But the meds and the stress of my health issues . . .

"Have you heard back from your architect friend yet? You didn't answer my text."

"Oh, sorry. I've been, ah, busy."

She's totally hiding something. But why?

She keeps talking. "He messaged me yesterday because he has to do some research. We scheduled a video chat for tomorrow."

"Awesome. So why are you avoiding me?"

She laughs but the sound is forced and awkward.

"You can't lie to me." I tap her on the hand.

"I can't lie to anyone." She leans closer, infiltrating my space, so near I breathe in the scent of wildflowers. "B, please don't press me on this. I've just . . . needed some space."

I lean back, struck dumb by her request. I'm not sure if I'm hurt or intrigued. Or both.

"B" is the nickname we use in our notes to each other. The term of endearment we share eases the sting of her words a little. I wish she would tell me what's going on with her, but I don't have the right to press.

"Okay. Show me what we're doing here."

She gives me a relieved smile and then we spend the next couple of hours working on details, making phone calls, and setting up photo shoots.

Then we call people who've sponsored the event in the past and get leads on more possible donors and people who might want to advertise in her calendar.

We run into an issue with vendors for food. No way to have decent food catered at this point.

"What about food trucks?" Bethany suggests.

"That's a good idea. My friend Scarlett is starting up a dessert truck. The extra publicity would be great."

She makes a note in her planner. "Do you have her number?"

"I can get it."

She nods and drops her pen. "My brain is fried."

"Maybe we can get some food and head home."

"Sounds good." She glances over to where Charlie and Angela are still working and then does a double take.

I follow her gaze. Angela and Charlie are in the midst of a fairly intense, close conversation, completely unaware of everyone around them.

Then Angela laughs and puts a hand on Charlie's shoulder and the smile they share is . . . well, it's . . .

Are they —? Wait. No. Are they *flirting*?

I whip my eyes back to Bethany and find her watching me. She's smiling.

"Someone's hitting it off," she murmurs.

I glance back over at them. I swear they're exchanging numbers, smiling and blushing at each other like high school kids.

A grin spreads over my face.

This might be the best news I've heard all week.

Chapter Twelve

It isn't the mountains ahead to climb that wear you out, it's the pebble in your shoe.
–Muhammad Ali

Bethany

"I did some digging around and got the plans for your building."

"That's amazing." My gaze slides to Brent.

He came over after training, hair still wet, dressed simply in athletic shorts and a white T-shirt. One muscular arm is draped on the back of the couch while he leans back, as gorgeous as ever.

The strain of his biceps against the cotton of his shirt draws my gaze. He's so delicious. I want to bite him. But I manage to restrain myself.

His face is a bit drawn, though. Is he still tired? We went to bed early last night. Maybe training is wiping him out.

I focus on the video on my phone.

"I'll email you a copy," Sam says. "I'm still not convinced it isn't air in the pipes. Maybe your super lied because they didn't want to deal with it, but anyway, I found something interesting. It appears there might be a dumbwaiter behind where your closet is."

"A dumb-a-whatta now?"

"Dumbwaiter. They're these old mini elevators for shifting objects up and down flights. Like food, laundry, that kind of stuff. They were pretty common in pre-war era apartments. But having space in your walls should be helping to block noises from outside, not creating additional sounds, unless there's something living in there. Maybe some rats have gotten into the hollow spots. If I'm reading your floor plan right, it's behind where the closet is now, and since you said that's where the banging is coming from, I would start there."

"Thanks, Sam. I owe you one."

"You owe me two. I also have an intern doing some research on the history of your building. Maybe these kinds of things have been reported before Gwen lived there. I'll let you know if anything interesting comes up. So, speaking of owing me, uh, is Brent around, by chance?"

I make a concerted effort not to glance over to where Brent's sitting. "No, he's got more important things to do than hang around with me. He's very busy and important."

Sam frowns. "Yeah, that's what I thought."

"Why do you ask?"

"No reason. You know, there's no reason at all I would maybe want to meet only the best tight end of the last two seasons or anything."

"You like him that much, huh?"

"Bethany." The phone moves closer so he can give me his intense look but I just end up getting a close-up shot of his nostril. "He's like the best thing that's happened to football in at least a decade. He's a six-four wall of man muscle. He has the best passing distance in the league and awesome hair. I would leave Gemma for him."

101

"Would you really?" I clear my throat. "You know, that's really funny because he's actually sitting right here." I turn the phone to put Brent's face in the screen.

I can no longer see Sam's expression clearly, which is unfortunate.

It must be good because Brent grins and tries to smother a chuckle. "Hey man, thanks for all your help. I really appreciate the support, too. It's always nice to meet a real fan."

There's silence on the other end and I can't help but crack up. I'm laughing so hard, I almost drop the phone.

"Bethany!" Sam barks.

"Yep?" I ask through giggles.

"Turn. The phone. Around."

I adjust the phone to face me and immediately burst into laughter again.

Sam's gone white. He shuts his eyes and shakes his head. "I can't believe you did that to me," he whispers.

Brent bites his lips, trying to hold in his laughter.

"You said you wanted to meet him."

"That's it. I'm going full-throttle pranks on your ass. You'll never be safe in this town again."

I laugh. "Bye, Sam, thanks for your help. I'll get Brent to send you a jersey."

"If you make that happen, I might forgive you, but I doubt it. I hope your ass gets haunted for the rest of your life. Don't ever ask me for help again, you horrible human. You will pay for your crimes against humanity."

I'm still laughing when he ends the call.

Brent releases a crack of laughter. "That was great. Give me his address and I'll send him one of our promo packages with a signed jersey and a few cards or something."

"That would be amazing. Although he's still going to find a way to get back at me. Sam's a real prankster."

"It's worth it for the laugh alone. You have no idea how much I needed that."

"Let's go see if we can find the dumb dumbwaiter."

We head to the hallway together and open up the closet door. I yank on the cord to illuminate the small space. We pull out the clothes hanging up and toss them onto the dresser out in the hallway.

Brent steps in first, his bulky frame taking up a significant portion of the space. He raps on the walls with a knuckle, both of us listening for an echo.

It isn't until he reaches the very back of the closet that I hear it—a hollow knock.

"I bet this is it," he says.

"It's all drywall. There's no way to get back there without breaking through the wall." I glance around, looking into the corners. "Maybe there's a latch like one of those old movies." I slip further into the closet, bringing me right next to Brent.

He inhales sharply when my hip grazes his.

Swallowing, I attempt to focus on the task at hand, but I am supremely aware of him. I mean, he's huge. And the closet is teeny tiny. His cologne tickles my nose, his masculine scent threading into my head and wrapping its tendrils around my suddenly heated insides. I inhale slowly.

"It is here?" I ask, resting a hand next to his.

His breathing hitches when our fingers brush.

I glance up to meet his eyes and find him watching me.

His vivid blue eyes are heated and focused on my lips.

My own breathing falters. He's taking up my vision, sucking the air out of the small space. It feels like he's everywhere, making it all too easy to imagine him all around me because, well, he is. What would it be like to have him over me? Under me? All that strength and power. The thought makes my stomach heat and thighs clench.

And then his phone chirps in his pocket.

His eyes shut and he swallows hard. "Sorry, I have to take this," he mutters. In one smooth movement he steps away.

"Hello? Yeah, that's me. . ."

That's all I catch of his conversation because the front door opens and shuts gently.

I frown. He had to leave the apartment entirely? I shake my head. It's none of my business.

The tiny closet feels like a huge empty space. I continue feeling around for a crack in the plaster, trying to focus on the task at hand instead of the strange moment with Brent.

"Hey."

I jump at the sound of his voice behind me.

"I've got to take off. I'll see you later, back at the apartment?"

"Yeah, of course. I'm going to talk to the super about the dumbwaiters. Maybe they can figure out where it leads. If there's an access point somewhere or something."

"Right. Let me know."

With a small wave and an even smaller smile, he's gone.

Weird.

It's probably because I was practically all over him in the closet and we're just friends and he's completely revolted by me.

Although I can't help but wonder . . . what was that call about?

~*~

104

Two hours later I'm dealing with my own annoying phone calls.

Mom.

She's called me about ten times, rapid-fire.

This is what she does when she's been drinking. Worse than a telemarketer. And it's always about something inane, like she needs the number for the movie theater or have I been to the dentist this year.

I can't deal with her right now. A twinge of guilt flickers through me, but if it were a real emergency, she would leave a message.

I didn't answer my phone because I was on the other line with the super. He knows nothing about dumbwaiters but promises to look into it and let me know.

I'm not holding my breath.

Brent is MIA the entire rest of the day and I use the time to call Freya. She's always good for a distraction.

"Hey, sexy girlfriend!" she yells as she answers the phone.

I laugh. "I'm not feeling terribly sexy at the moment."

"Oh, no. Did you get mugged in Central Park? Did someone on the subway get handsy? Did you scream that Chicago pizza is better in a crowded room and get shanked by a local?"

I laugh. "Not quite. Didn't Ted tell you?"

"Tell me what? That you're *not* banging the tight end for the New York Sharks? Nope. He totally didn't tell me that."

I huff. "Banging isn't happening."

"Ah ha, that's why you don't feel sexy. Doesn't he know about your magical vag?"

"Clearly not. Maybe you should tell him."

She laughs. "Maybe Gwen already has. Remember when she came over and we were harassing you about being a super slut?"

"How could I forget?"

"Maybe we should have told her it's a term of endearment and doesn't necessarily mean you have multiple STDs and a blown-out vagina."

"Dude. You should not speak those words again, ever."

"So seriously though, tell me everything."

I explain all that's happened since the last time we talked, about how Brent has been helping me figure out the apartment stuff and what Sam told me.

"Your life is so much more exciting than mine."

"I doubt that. How's Dean?"

"Dreamy as usual."

There's a knock at the door. "Hold on," I tell Freya.

It's Natalie.

"It's my neighbor's girlfriend. I'll call you back."

We hang up and I open the door.

"Hey, Natalie."

She's wearing a pale blouse embroidered with brightly colored robins. Where do they find these bird clothes?

"Martha made you a casserole," she says by way of greeting.

"That's . . . so nice."

Natalie laughs. "It's okay, I made sure she didn't do anything crazy. Her dementia is pretty bad, so I've been helping Steven watch her before we eat her cooking."

I take the dish from her. "Thank you."

"It's tater tot casserole."

"I love tater tots." Did I tell Steven about my love for the tots before? I can't remember half the things that spew out of my mouth. "Did you want to come in?" I step back to invite her, but she shakes her head.

"Thanks, but I better get back. Steven's at work and I offered to hang out with Martha until he gets off."

She leaves and while I'm sticking the casserole in the fridge, my cell starts ringing.

Damn, I'm popular today. But I don't recognize the number.

"Hello?"

"Hi. I'm looking for Bethany Connell?" The woman's voice is crisp and professional.

"This is she."

"This is Samantha calling from NV Energy account services."

"Um. Okay."

"The automatic deduction for your address at 1013 Sky Avenue was rejected. Would you like to make a payment with another card and add a new payment account to your records?"

Mom's house. Is that why she kept calling me? "That can't be possible. I had enough money in that account yesterday to cover it."

"You might need to contact your bank. In the meantime, can you provide us with another card to avoid late charges?"

"Yeah. Sure."

It takes a few minutes to get my purse and pull out a credit card to give them.

My mind is racing the whole time. I know I had enough in there to last the rest of the month and part of next. What happened?

As soon as I hang up with the utility company, I call the bank and move into the living room so I have more room to pace.

The rep sounds like a co-ed from Southern California. Every sentence ends on a high note like it's a question, with the word "like" peppered throughout. It's a sharp contrast to her words.

"So, like, a large sum was withdrawn late last night?"

Money was taken? From my account? She goes on about how there's, "like, less than a dollar left in your checking and savings and there will be, like, a service charge for maintaining a low balance long-term."

"But . . ." I find my voice. "I haven't taken out any large withdrawals. Where was it taken out?"

"You have, like, a second card holder?"

Oh shit. *Mom*.

She's listed on the account for emergencies. I had a second debit card, but I lost it in the move.

Or I left it behind.

And then she found it.

I groan, frustration filling my veins with fire. Voice shaking, I have the rep remove Mom's name and cancel the card. Not that it matters. The damage has been done.

I want to cry. Sob. Shake my fist at the universe that gave me a mother who can't handle being an adult.

Instead, I hang up with the bank and call the source of all my problems.

"Hey, baby," she answers, happy and tipsy.

It makes my blood boil over.

I hope she remembers this. "Mom. Why did you take all my money? No, don't answer, I know why you did it."

She must hear the anger in my voice. There's a slight hesitation, and then the defensiveness starts. "I didn't do anything wrong. It's my money, too."

My teeth grit around my words. "Here's the thing. It's really not. I removed your name from the account and the card is canceled. I'm calling everyone now and removing my accounts from your utilities, and I'm not paying your property taxes or buying you food anymore. You're on your own."

Silence down the line for about three long seconds.

"You can't do that! I am your mother! I gave birth to you. I raised you."

And here's the guilt trip. But I've heard it all before. Too many times. "Yeah, well, I've been going through the pain of reverse childbirth to you for the last ten years and I'm done."

"How am I supposed to live?"

"I don't know, Mother. You can use the retirement check you get every month."

"It's not enough to live on."

"It would be if you stopped spending it on booze."

She's quiet and then the wrenching sobs begin. "I can't believe you're cutting me off like this. Aren't you ashamed of yourself? You're going to drive me to drink even more."

Blaming her drinking on everyone but herself. I used to feel bad for her, but I think I've run out of the emotion. "I'm not ashamed. I'm not forcing you to do anything. But I am sorry, Mom. Sorry I let you leech off me for so long. Sorry Dad died and you felt you had to escape everything, including me. Sorry you've let your addiction ruin our relationship. But I'm not sorry for this. I should have done it a long time ago. When you get sober, you can call me. Otherwise, don't bother."

I hang up and burst into tears.

Chapter Thirteen

I think that the good and the great are only separated by the willingness to sacrifice.
–Kareem Abdul-Jabbar

Brent

I haven't signed the contract yet.

In the afternoon, I meet with Roger. I manage to fake enthusiasm and then put him off by telling him I want to talk to Dad about it.

Yeah right, like I would tell him anything.

I'm panicking. The MRI confirmed the results of the 2-D echo, like my doctor had suspected. She pushed me again for surgery and I told her I would call later to schedule it. Everything I do is just a delaying tactic for the inevitable.

I promised to face my demons and still . . . I let them freeze me.

It's early evening and thankfully Bethany is home when I get there.

The most welcome distraction of my day.

She's in the living room in her PJs. There's a carton of ice cream on the table and she's trying to balance a spoon on her nose.

I laugh. "What are you doing?"

"This is much harder than it looks."

"I'm sure. You left some ice cream on it."

"Oh." She pulls the spoon from her face, leaving a smear of cream behind, and sticks the spoon in her mouth to clean it.

She's not trying to be sexy. There's ice cream on her nose. But her pink lips closing around the spoon make my mouth water anyway.

"C'mere. Try it."

I sit in front of her on the floor and she tries to balance the spoon for me, moving slowly and leaning in close before gently placing the curved part on the tip of my nose.

She's focusing hard, her tongue sticking slightly out the corner of her mouth, food still on her face, and I crack up.

The spoon clatters to the floor.

"Stop laughing!"

I laugh harder.

She falls back on the floor, groaning. Her shirt rides up, exposing a sliver of smooth skin.

I swallow. "Have you been drinking?"

She sits up, tugging her shirt down, her expression chagrined. "I had a can of wine. I don't normally because my—" She cuts off with a cough, then takes a drink of water from the glass on the table. "But I just . . . today was hard."

"A can of wine, huh?"

She shrugs. "I'm real classy like that."

"What happened?"

"Well, the good news is the super found something."

"What did he find?"

I notice the misdirection and the sentence chopping, but I don't comment. There's something going on with Bethany that she clearly doesn't want to share. I understand the sentiment, even though I wish she would confide in me. But the apartment haunting is a safe topic.

"The dumbwaiter goes all the way to the basement, by the laundry room. It's obvious someone's been in there. It's all cleared of dust and cobwebs. Someone has been using the pulley system. The original paneling for the opening to my apartment has been built over, but there's a latch from the inside of the dumbwaiter and they found a crack in the corner of my closet. Someone has been creeping in there. Why? Who knows! Because I'm cursed. Anyway, they boarded it up temporarily, and they're getting a contractor to pour concrete over the entrance within the next few days. So I can move back. You don't have to deal with me anymore."

"I like dealing with you."

"Yeah, right."

"So you're resorting to canned wine because you're cursed?"

"And because your father is a poop taco."

I groan. "What did he do now?"

She leans toward me. We're sitting cross-legged on the floor, facing each other like kindergartners.

"I keep setting up interviews with these amazing applicants, and he keeps running them off."

"I wish I could say that info is surprising. What's he doing now?"

"Well one woman was slightly overweight and he asked her when the baby was due and if it would interfere with her job."

I shut my eyes and shake my head. "Oh, no."

"Oh, yes. But wait, it gets worse. He had a list. I think he got them from a website about questions you absolutely cannot ask during interviews. There were some about religion, sexual preference, age . . . All the biggest no-nos in the HR world, he tapped into it. I had to talk people out of suing. He's a tyrant."

I lean closer and rub her shoulders. They were getting progressively higher and tighter as she told the story.

Her eyes fall shut. She moans and leans into my hands. "I'll give you thirty minutes to stop doing that."

I swallow. I should stop this. In a couple minutes.

In the meantime, I take advantage of the moment to watch her with her eyes closed. Her head tilts to the side and my gaze trips down the slope of her neck and stops right where it meets her shoulders. I rub a thumb over the spot. She's so soft. I want to bite her, right there. Her mouth opens slightly. It would be so easy to lean in and sample her mouth. What would she taste like? Vanilla ice cream? Wildflowers and sugar?

Before my thoughts make me completely lose it, I remove my hands with a final pat. "I've got an idea. You're calling in tomorrow. We could both use a break and it can be like our own little goodbye party since you won't be my roomie anymore."

"What? I can't take time off. I'll get fired."

"Hasn't he already fired you like fourteen times?"

"More like forty. He gets mad when I don't agree with him on everything, but the truth is he wants me to disagree with him. He's just ornery."

"Trust me. He can't live without you. You've burrowed your way into the company faster than anyone I've ever seen. He can't fire you and I won't let him. I'll call him myself if I have to. You've been working too hard. At the office and now on the charity game. You need a break, a mental health day. I'll take care of everything. All you have to do is wear comfortable shoes."

She purses her pink lips at me. "I'll agree if you promise not to go all crazy and spend a bunch of money. That will just lead to guilt. And then I'll feel even worse and I'll drink even more and you'll have to check me in

113

to Betty Ford, and then the press will run stories about how you turned me into a major druggie cult member."

I laugh. "Well that progressed quickly. Fine. You got it. Scout's honor. Everything we do tomorrow will be free or cheap. But you have to be ready to go by seven."

She straightens. "Wait, in the morning?"

~*~

I'm ready with coffee by six thirty, feeling more upbeat and positive than I have all week. I'm excited to show Bethany around my city and see her reactions to everything. But it's more than that. I love spending time with her. Except it's getting harder and harder not to take her in my arms and kiss her.

She emerges from the bedroom at six fifty-five with a zombie-like moan. "Coffeeee."

I hand her a cup as she comes into the kitchen, which she takes without comment.

She's wearing a soft long-sleeved shirt with a large neck that exposes one shoulder. Her hair is a mess of curls and she's the most delicious thing I've ever seen, even with puffy eyes and a tired face.

She takes a sip of the coffee, leaning back against the counter and eying me.

I glance down to see what she's looking at. I'm dressed simply in jeans, a long-sleeved grey Henley, and an old-school pair of Vans.

"After you get ready, we need sustenance." I rub my hands together.

She lifts a brow. "Are you on the menu?" Immediately, her hand claps over her mouth and her cheeks flush.

Laughter bubbles out of me. I was thinking something similar a minute ago. "I think your filter is broken." I give into the urge to reach over and push a lock of her wild hair behind her ear. The fleeting touch of her soft skin sends a frisson of yearning through my body.

I want so much I can't have.

And why can't I have? Would it really be so bad to consider more? I know Bethany is attracted to me and we have fun together. Would it be so horrible?

Although, she's been vocally averse to being "date-y" with me from the get-go.

And then there are my medical issues. But what if her thoughts have changed now that we know each other? And what if I told her everything? Would she run? Could I blame her if she did? I can barely face my own demons. How can I expect someone I care about to face them with me?

"It's because it's early," she whines and drags my thoughts back to the moment. "How are you so happy and energetic?" She squints at me. "Satan?"

I chuckle. "Don't worry. I'll feed you and you'll be as good as new. You're going to eat what all good New Yorkers eat in the morning: a bagel from a cart. Now hurry up and get dressed and I'll make you more coffee."

She frowns at me but saunters down the hall anyway. "Fine, fine, I'm going, I'm going," she mutters.

She reemerges ten minutes later in form-fitting jeans and a T-shirt, looking much more awake and a lot less cranky.

"I'm ready for my tour, Mr. Lord of the Underworld."

115

"Good. The River Styx awaits you, my lady," I say as I'm opening the door for her.

We leave the Porsche behind. "No having to deal with parking," I explain. "We're using cabs and subway only."

"What if people recognize you?"

I shake my sunglasses at her before putting an Oakland hat on, making her laugh. "I'll definitely be incognito in this."

We stop for more coffee and the bagels I promised, and I make her try one with lox.

"Is that fish?" She wrinkles her nose.

"You have to try it. It's like a New York institution."

From there, it's a whirlwind of sightseeing.

The early spring morning is brisk and bright, and I use the chill in the air as an excuse to stay close to Bethany, our arms bumping periodically as we walk.

We go to Times Square, already bustling with activity. We stop on the pedestrian walkway in the center and she eyes the activity around us as I watch her. I don't have to look to know what she's seeing: brightly colorful billboards, zipper news crawls, a giant wooden art installation in the shape of a ship. The sounds of traffic accompany the view, the hum of tires on the pavement mingling with the occasional honk.

"Times Square is sometimes referred to as the center of the universe and the heart of the world," I tell her. "It got its current name in 1904 when *The New York Times* moved its headquarters into the Times building." I point out the tall building. "The Times isn't there anymore. Now it's where they drop the ball on New Year's Eve."

Bethany claps her hands together. "You're going to tell me some history, too? This is the best tour ever."

I grin. "It was originally called Longacre Square after Long Acre in London, because it was a big mecca for horse and carriage trading."

116

"I can't imagine this place covered in horses. Or grass."

From there, we take the subway to Broadway to see the fearless girl. I get a picture of Bethany facing down the bull with her lips pursed and her eyes crossed.

"*Charging Bull* was installed in 1989 by Arturo Di Modica. When Kristen Visbal was commissioned to install *Fearless Girl*, Di Modica was pretty pissed."

"Why?"

"It was an advertising shtick, and she turned the bull into a bad guy when it's supposed to be a symbol of strength."

"Hm. I like both of them. A bull doesn't have to be a villain. He could be like Ferdinand." She pats the sculpture on the head. "He totally looks like he wants to sniff the flowers."

It's a quick walk—less than ten minutes—from there to the Staten Island Ferry.

"It's free?" she asks, eyes wide while we rush through the stale smell of fast food across the terminal to make the next ferry.

"Absolutely. And it runs every thirty minutes, twenty-four hours a day."

"It's huge," she gasps as we walk the pathway onto the giant orange boat. "I thought it would be like a little tugboat or something."

Her reactions are everything I thought they would be, wide-eyed wonder and enthusiasm. It makes the whole experience that much more thrilling for me—like I'm seeing it all again for the first time.

I make sure we get a good viewing spot on the east-facing side. We stand on the deck and sail past the Statue of Liberty. "Best view of the statue in the city," I tell her.

The wind whips her curls back and she watches me with bright, excited eyes, the tip of her nose already turning a little red from the brisk March breeze. "Tell me all the things."

I set my elbows against the railing and lean toward her. The view of Bethany's smile is better than anything else we've seen today. "The statue's full name is 'Liberty Enlightening the World.' "

"Doesn't quite roll off the tongue, does it?"

"Lady Liberty wears a size 879 shoe."

"You know what they say about women with big feet."

"What do they say?"

"Big toes."

I laugh, rolling my eyes. "You're ridiculous."

"Yep. You're just now figuring this out? Next factoid, please."

"Visitors have to climb 354 stairs to reach the crown."

"Thank God we took the ferry."

I point to Ellis Island as the boat plows onward. "Ellis Island was used for pirate hangings in the early 1800s."

"Pirates," she gasps and leans closer, lowering her voice like she's telling me a secret. "What did the pirate say when he blew out his candles on his eightieth birthday?"

"What?"

"Aye matey!" She nudges me with her elbow, totally cracking herself up.

I chuckle and lean into her bright laughter, soaking it up like the rays of the sun. This is why Bethany is like no other person I've ever met. She so inherently silly and fun and just so much *herself*. There's no trying to impress or act mature or rich or self-important.

"Tell me more stuff," she insists.

"It opened as an immigration port in 1892. Almost 450,000 immigrants were processed during the first year."

"Damn. That's amazing."

"The busiest day ever at Ellis Island was April 17, 1907. Over eleven thousand people arrived. They say about forty percent of the current population can trace their ancestry to immigrants who arrived at Ellis Island."

We spend more time talking and I tell her all the little factoids I've researched and she tells me lame pirate jokes.

"How do pirates know that they're pirates?"

"How?"

"They think, therefore they arrrgh."

I laugh.

She smiles at my response, her eyes lighting up. "You have the best laugh."

"I think I've laughed more in the last three weeks than I have in my entire life."

Her head tilts. "How do you know all this trivia? Do they make you take a New York–specific history class when you grow up here?"

"Not exactly. I might have stayed up a little late last night researching some of this stuff."

And maybe glanced at my phone a few times while she wasn't looking.

"You did?" Her eyes widen and then shift down to the water flowing past the boat, white-tipped waves as breaking against the boat. She turns her gaze back to mine. "Why do you do all these things for me?"

"What do you mean?"

"I mean, you've helped me with my crazy problems, you let me stay at your place, you know when I need a break and make it happen, you bought me a night-light, and now you've stayed up late memorizing facts just so

I'll have a good time. I don't think even my best friend would go through so much trouble for me."

My tongue sticks to the roof of my mouth but I force it into action.

It's time to tell her the full truth.

Chapter Fourteen

I'd rather regret the risks that didn't work out than the chances I didn't take at all.
–Simone Biles

Bethany

He takes a breath and glances away from me, out to the sea.

His jaw is tight and I think maybe he's going to ignore my question but then he pulls his sunglasses off and sticks them on top of his hat. His gaze returns to mine and his eyes are bright and open.

"Bethany, the truth is . . . I like you."

I blink. "Well, I like you, too."

"No." He bites his lip. "The feelings I have for you go beyond friendly." He's watching my reaction, his intense blue gaze searing into mine.

My heart stutters in my chest and my breathing accelerates. "But we . . . what . . . why?"

He chuckles and shakes his head, his eyes leaving mine for the water beyond, squinting into the light glancing off the waves. "I can't believe I just said that. It sounds so lame. But you've always been honest with me and you deserve same. It's okay if you don't feel what I do. I don't expect anything from you other than your friendship. I know you don't want to date me—you've been perfectly clear about that from the beginning—so if

I've just totally freaked you out, we can pretend this conversation never happened."

I think I've gone into shock.

Brent Crawford is a rambling mess of nerves. The most gorgeous man I've ever laid eyes on. The one who could have any woman in New York and probably the entire planet, if not the universe. He likes me? Likes . . . *me*? Crazy-haired, unfiltered-mouth, needy, ghost-ridden me?

It can't be true.

I pinch him.

"Ow. Why'd you do that?"

"I wanted to make sure I wasn't dreaming."

His smile is wry. "I think you're supposed to pinch yourself."

I nod. "I'll try that next time." And before I can overthink it and totally screw it up, I reach up on my toes, grab his face, and pull him to me.

His lips are firm but soft, slack with surprise initially, but then his hands tunnel into my hair and he pulls me closer. His movements are abrupt but his touch is surprisingly tender. Like he wants me so badly but he doesn't want to break me. Like he's the pirate and I'm his treasure and despite his greed I must be plundered with soft fingers and gentle touches. His hat tilts off his head, falling behind him along with his sunglasses, but we ignore it. His tongue is warm and insistent against mine and holy hell the man can kiss. A pulse of need trips through my body and I tug him closer, pressing myself against him to bring more of our bodies together.

And that's when he pulls back. "I . . . don't want to rush things." The unsteady tremor in his voice and his arm around my shoulder soothe the sting of his withdrawal just when it was getting interesting.

I nod. He's right. My legs are trembling and my stomach is hot with want. "Right. Totally. No rushing.

That's smart." I glance around the boat, looking for somewhere private. Maybe I could convince him to do it in the bathroom. There's gotta be a janitor's closet somewhere.

"B." A gentle finger on my jaw pulls my gaze back to his. "You're looking for somewhere for us to hook up, aren't you?"

"Are you a mind reader?"

"Your face is like a book." He chuckles, and I swear there is a thread of nerves in the sound. "I'm serious about you. This isn't about an easy lay. You mean more to me than a quick orgasm on a dirty ferry."

I grin. "I don't really see anything wrong with a quick orgasm on a dirty ferry. Maybe someday we can try it? After we've exhausted all other ways of orgasming, of course."

He laughs at the comment, but his jaw tenses and once again I get the sense that I'm missing something.

His arm is around my neck and he pulls me into his side, kissing the top of my head.

It almost convinces me I'm imagining the underlying tension.

~*~

We spend the rest of the day like real tourists, eating hot dogs at Coney Island, going on a couple of rides at Luna Park, and exploring The Met. Brent buys us matching *I heart NY* T-shirts. We put them on over the shirts we're already wearing and even though it looks lumpy and weird, he kisses my nose and tells me I'm adorable.

And I almost believe it. His eyes are constantly on me, running over my body with enjoyment that he's no longer trying to hide.

It takes a while to get back to his apartment because there's a mechanical issue on the Q but I don't mind because Brent and I hold hands and he plays with my fingers, sending shots of energy straight to the butterflies dancing in my stomach. Conversation is easy and fun and I never want this day to end.

There's one last stop, but he takes me back to the apartment to change into something warmer and to pick up the car.

He tells me to keep it casual so I trade out my T-shirts for a thin sweater since it's getting colder as the sun sets.

"Where are we going?"

"The one place we missed."

"I'm sure we missed more than one place."

"One very iconic New York location. I'll give you hints."

"Ooh yay. What do I get if I guess right?"

"What do you want?"

I bite my lip and pretend to think about it. "Anything I want?"

He turns away, pushing the button on the elevator. "Uh, almost anything." He smiles at me, but there's strain in the tension of his jaw and the line of his broad shoulders.

I tilt my head at him.

"Your first clue is that this place was named one of the seven wonders of the modern world by the American Society of Civil Engineers." He takes my hand, his thumb running over my knuckles, and the motion soothes away my insecurities.

I'm about to make another joke about how it must be in his pants and we don't really have to go anywhere, but I manage to restrain myself. "Is it the naked cowboy?"

"Close, but no. It's also the most photographed building in the world."

"A building, huh?"

He grimaces as we step off the elevator into the lobby. "That totally gives it away, doesn't it?"

"Pretty much, but I'll pretend I don't know you're taking me to the most romantic place in the world so we can keep playing."

He feeds me more bits of information while we drive down Third Avenue, through Gramercy Park and past the brownstones and upscale apartment buildings.

"It's home to so many businesses it has its own zip code."

"Seriously? That's insane."

We find parking eventually and walk to the building.

The lobby of the Empire State Building is crowded with people, their voices echoing against marble walls. A golden ceiling etched with cogs and wheels glows above our heads and I keep glancing up as we walk through the crowd.

"They're open every day of the year until two in the morning," Brent continues. We bypass the line and he waves at a guard at one of the shiny elevators.

Some people in line murmur and flash photos as we pass. He forgot his hat.

"Seriously? So when Tom Hanks finally met Meg Ryan at the top of the Empire State Building, it was past two a.m.?"

"Apparently so."

"Can we reenact the final scene at the top?"

He chuckles. "If you really want to."

I clap my hands. "Best date ever!"

"Hey Superman," the guard says when we reach the elevator. He and Brent perform some kind of complicated handshake. Then Brent hands him an envelope. "You're the best." The guard slips the envelope into his jacket, then punches a code on the elevator keypad. The doors slide open.

"Thank you for getting us in at the last minute." Brent glances down at me. "This is Bethany." There's a slight hesitation before he says my name. Not sure whether to use the *g* word?

It is confusing. What are we? He said he liked me, but that doesn't necessarily mean we're boyfriend and girlfriend. Does it? It sounds like such a juvenile title. Girlfriend. Like something you have in middle school, not when you're nearly thirty.

We step onto the lift and the guard reaches in to push some more buttons for us before giving me a wink. "Nice to meet you. You kids have fun now."

The doors shut and the elevator begins to rise.

"Is it going to take us to the observation deck?"

"Not quite. We're going a little farther than that."

The elevator opens and we walk out onto a window-enclosed observatory that spans the perimeter of the building.

"This is the 102nd floor. But we're not stopping here."

We make a hard right turn, where another employee in a suit smiles at Brent and opens a door to our left. A narrow, dark staircase leads up.

I lift my brows at Brent. "Is this where you commit the perfect crime?"

He laughs. "No, but that's not a bad idea."

He lets me go first and we walk up the stairs. It opens into a wider space with exposed copper pipes and another staircase.

"Are we going up more?" I ask.

"No. Not allowed. The hatch there," he points, "leads to the antenna. We're going here." He opens a windowed door and we step out onto a narrow walk space. There's a thick, waist-high white wall and a matching handrail. Beyond, the entire city sparkles beneath us.

"Holy shit." I walk to the ledge and look down and immediately feel dizzy. I step back and nearly collide with Brent.

"I gotcha." His hands are warm and he wraps an arm around my shoulders.

"This is . . . amazing." I glance around. The walkway runs in a narrow circle around the spire, which looms above us. "Is anyone else here?"

"No. This is a little New York secret. They only let a select few up here. Welcome to the 103rd floor."

"The perks of being famous."

He shrugs and the movement runs through me. "I'm sure journalists and press sometimes, too."

"I think I saw Taylor Swift post a pic from up here once."

"Probably. Let's check it out."

We circle the building and it's the most amazing and terrifying thing I've ever experienced. The cold wind whips my hair around my face, turning the tip of my nose numb, but Brent's hand is warm in mine.

He puts his jacket on my shoulders while we absorb the view.

Everything looks tiny, like we're in an airplane without the restricted view. He points out the Chrysler Building, the spire glowing like a candle. Times Square is easy to spot, the colorful buildings all alight in blues and greens and yellows.

"What bridge is that?" I point to the structure aglow with traffic and lights amongst the columns.

"Williamsburg, I think."

Once we've seen everything and I'm shivering despite the borrowed jacket, he guides me back inside and we head down a floor to the enclosed space of the 102nd floor.

There's no one else here. Just us and the view out the window.

A bag of food and a bottle of wine are waiting for us next to a blanket.

"Wow. You planned a picnic?"

He rubs a hand along the back of his head. "Too cheesy?"

"No. It's perfect." I swallow. No one's ever gone to as much trouble as Brent has, as he continues to do, even when he barely knew me.

"What's in the bag?" I sniff. "Wait, don't tell me. Chicken nuggets and tater tots."

He laughs. "You can smell that?"

"Am I right?" I grab his arm in excitement.

"You have a nose like a shark."

"That's a compliment. Sharks are awesome."

"They sure are. Way better than Oakland." He rolls his eyes and I laugh.

"Blasphemer."

"I brought chocolate cake, too."

I can't contain my smile. "Forgiven."

We eat the chicken fingers and tater tots with our fingers and sip our wine out of plastic cups.

Brent is affectionate while we eat, feeding me one of his tots, kissing a spot of ketchup from my lips.

It's a little confusing. I mean, I know he wants to take it slow, but I can't help but wonder why he seems so wary about the physical stuff.

What if he's a virgin?

No. No way.

Twice now we've woken up together, spooned together like lovers. He was never aroused. Maybe he has

128

a super tiny penis and he's insecure about it. Or maybe, more likely, he's just not attracted to me. But if that were true, why all the kissing and affection? It doesn't make sense.

I have to figure it out.

There's a lull in our conversation when he's pulling out the chocolate cake and forks, and I use it to plant my investigative seeds.

"How long were you and Bella together?"

"Since high school."

Damn. My longest relationship was with a box of wine. I nearly inhale my drink. "That's a really long time. Like a decade."

He hands me a fork and puts the small circle of cake between us. "Yeah. I know. That's why it was so shocking when she broke it off after I started doing well with football. I really thought she was the one. But she couldn't handle my job. She was insecure about our relationship and for a long time I thought it was my fault, but I never did anything for her to lose faith in me. She gave me an ultimatum and I didn't choose her."

Maybe that's why he seemed so down and out when I first met him.

I take a bite of cake and moan. "This is so good. How long ago did you break up?"

"It's been . . . over a year. Once she left, I moved in with Marc. That's when all the insanity happened with Marissa and Gwen."

"You know, I guess I could kind of see where Bella was coming from. Being in a relationship with a celebrity would be hard. You travel during the season. Women stalk you, throw themselves at you . . . it would be hard to believe one person could be enough."

He takes a bite of cake. I watch his lips press against the fork before meeting his eyes. There's a small crease between his brows. "Are you having second thoughts?"

"About what?"

"Us."

I put my fork down. "Are we an us?"

"I would like to be. I thought I was pretty clear."

I purse my lips and pretend to think about it. "You've been sort of clear."

He leans forward and gives me a soft kiss, making my pout melt. Just a touch, a hint of chocolatey pleasure, and then he pulls back. "Your turn."

"For what?"

"I've given you my dirty history. Now you get to spill."

"Uh-huh, I'll show you mine if you show me yours?"

"Yep."

I swallow back a twinge of shame. I have nothing of value to share, so I keep my words light. "There's not much to tell. It's sort of embarrassing but I haven't had a lot of experience in long-term relationships. The last serious boyfriend I had was in high school."

"Really? I find that hard to believe."

"Why?"

"Because look at you. You're funny and smart and strong." His hand lifts to my face, cupping my cheek for a moment before falling away. "And you're beautiful."

I stare at him. No one's ever told me all that before. I have no idea how to respond. My initial inquisition goes out the window. I don't care if he's a man-whore or Mother Teresa or doesn't have a penis at all. Right now, he's mine.

"Well, there was one guy in college. I thought it could get serious. But then I overheard him talking to his buddies about how I wasn't good for anything more than a decent fuck."

"Are you kidding me? What an asshole."

"Right? The biggest. After that I was a bit hesitant to give anyone too much of my heart. My mom always told me I fall too fast and my heart's too soft to handle the break. So instead I ended up partying a lot. Maybe too much. It was a way to escape." And a way to avoid my problems at home.

"This guy really did a number on you."

I glance down at my lap. Sort of. Not really. I was escaping Mom more than anything else, but I'm not sharing those tender bits. I've never told anyone the whole truth. Not even my closest friends back home.

"Yeah . . . he really *fowled* me up." I nudge him with an elbow. "Get it? Fowl?"

He groans. "Are we doing bird puns again?"

We laugh. Crisis averted.

He leans in while I'm still smiling and presses his mouth against mine. It's a brief caress, a momentary brush of warmth and then he pulls back and his grin is sheepish. "I wanted to taste your smile."

My stomach flutters at his words, and I can't control myself. I ease against him and steal his lips, seeking more of his warmth, more of him. The brush of his mouth against mine sends a pulse of desire shooting downward. His lips are soft but persistent, and he tastes like chocolate cake. His hands slide into my hair, gentle but strong. He is a study in contrasts.

When his tongue slides past my lips, I melt against him and then we're tumbling back, lying on the ground facing each other, our mouths never leaving the other's even as we fall. An ache begins to build inside me, and I ease closer and closer, but it's not enough.

His hand runs down one arm to my hip, gripping me firmly.

I reciprocate the movement, clasping his hip, pressing myself closer against him.

He pulls back on a gasp.

"We should go somewhere more comfortable."

Oh, hell yeah.

My body is flush with heat.
Finally.

Chapter Fifteen

If you aren't going all the way, why go at all?
–Joe Namath

Brent

"Thank you for today. And dinner, and . . . everything." Bethany's hand on my arm is warm and soft. Her eyes are glazed and her lips are pink and swollen from our earlier make-out session.

"It was a great day."

We're standing in the space between the hall and the kitchen, stuck somewhere between need and anticipation and anxiety.

My body is buzzing. It has been all day. I want more than anything to take her into my arms, kiss her senseless, but I don't know if I'm ready. I know where it will lead—where she'll want it to lead—and I can't. Literally.

My heart speeds up in my chest.

Can I be the man she wants? The one she needs? I should tell her everything but the words get caught in my throat.

I need to come clean. It's why I stopped us at the Empire State Building. I need to tell her everything so she knows why, but . . . what if she doesn't want me? What if all my problems are a deal breaker?

I imagine her eyes growing cold. Distant. Pitying. Disappointed.

No.

She won't judge me.

Will she?

It could be a simple half-truth. One kiss. One moment and then I can pull away with the excuse of wanting to take her seriously, to take us seriously. It's not entirely a lie. I don't want to rush this thing between us, but the look in her eyes . . . I've already seen it. She'll think I don't want her.

Her eyes are on mine, wide and vulnerable and we've been staring at each other for longer than what should be comfortable but the taut wire of tension between us pulls us inexorably inward.

Her hands run up my arms, lightly squeezing. "Mother ducker," she murmurs, her fingers around my biceps.

I laugh softly. "Punny."

In the dim light of the hall, her eyes are dreamy and watching me like I'm the best dessert in the world and she can't wait to eat me. And I can't hold her back any longer.

The kiss is like a warm fire on a rainy day. I could lose myself in her lips forever.

I don't mean for the pressure between us to ramp up into a blaze. I want to keep it light and sweet, but I can't control my response when her fingers slip under my shirt, against the bare skin of my back.

Her warm hands trail to my stomach and the kiss turns insistent. The press of our mouths becomes harder, escalating into an inferno of clashing tongues. Her fingers explore up my stomach, pulling my shirt over my head and tossing it on the ground.

The momentary separation only makes us come back together harder. Her mouth is demanding and devouring and I love every second of it.

We somehow make it over to the couch, still kissing. She pulls me with only the force of her lips and the subtle tug of her hands. Before I can figure out what's happening, she pushes me down to a seat and straddles me, her lips on my neck for a brief and tantalizing suck before we're kissing again.

I moan into her mouth and my hand brushes up, under her shirt, feeling her through her bra before pulling the cup down so I can run a thumb over her already peaked nipple.

Her head falls back on a gasp. She feels amazing. Like nothing I've ever . . . Thoughts disappear under the strength of the need flooding through me.

My lips nibble down her neck and then she grinds against my lap, her fingers fumbling for the buttons.

All of my thoughts coalesce into panic.

"Wait." I grasp her wrists between us. "Stop."

Her body tenses against mine. I ease my grip on her hands and suck her bottom lip into my mouth.

"Please," I whisper against her lips. "Let me make you feel good first." There's a smidge of guilt attached to the words, knowing that it won't go any further. Can't go any further.

"Yes," she says just before our mouths meet again.

I slip her shirt over her head and chuck it to join mine on the floor.

Her breasts are spilling out of a satiny black bra. I can't pull my eyes away, her chest right at my eye line. I tug one cup down, exposing a tight pink nipple. I suck it into my mouth and her head falls back on a groan.

"Brent." She thrusts her hips in my direction, seeking relief that I cannot wait to provide—but not in that position.

I spin her around, settling her in my lap so her back is against my chest. I reach down between her legs, and delve into her pants.

She's not wearing underwear.

The realization pushes a groan from my chest and ignites a frantic yearning throughout my body, all the way to my toes.

I brush against her most sensitive spot, skating my fingers through her already wet folds.

With a gasp, she arches her back and turns her head to meet mine. I sip at her lips, slowing our movements while I slide my finger into her heat, pressing my palm against her clit and moving my fingers in time with my tongue. She moans, trembling in my arms, breasts pointed to the ceiling.

Holy fuck. She's the most beautiful thing I've ever laid eyes on.

I run a free hand up her chest to tug at her puckering nipples and I'm rewarded by a groan and her hips thrusting against my hand.

Her movements are intoxicating. Her moans and wildflower scent mixed with the heat of her arousal invades my senses and consumes my every thought until all that exists, all that matters are the slick sounds of her flesh and the hungry rock of her body clenched around my finger.

Her hand reaches down and covers mine, gripping me as I stroke and press into her a little harder, a little faster.

I glide in a second finger and her movements grow frantic.

Every whimper and thrust incites a matching thirst that makes my heart throb in my chest. She squirms as pleasure drums through her, creating an answering beat of pleasure within me, as if her body is my own.

And just like that, she explodes and shatters in my arms, pulsing around my fingers, surrendering to her release.

I want to bang my fists against my chest, howl at the moon, shout to the world.

Once the aftershocks quiver away she turns in my arms and burrows her face into my neck.

Our heavy pants fill the silence.

"That was . . . amazing." Her breath puffs against my neck.

"It really, really was." She has no idea.

She sits back in my lap and runs her hands down my chest, her eyes tracking the movement on my flesh and then she goes for the buttons of my pants. "My turn." The wicked grin she shoots me is nearly my undoing.

"Wait." For the second time, I still her hands.

I can't let this continue. I have to tell her, but I can't quite pull my thoughts together.

Her grin drops slowly, like the ball drop in Times Square, a full minute from top to bottom.

She swallows. "It's because of my dirty vagina, isn't it?"

A startled laugh breezes past my lips. "What? No. You don't have a dirty vagina." I can't help it. I laugh harder, the sound jangling with a touch of nerves since I'm about to tell her . . . everything.

"Stop laughing at my lady parts!"

"I'm not laughing at your parts. I'm laughing at your words. Come here."

I hug her to me, breathing in the wildflower scent of her hair for a few long seconds. Then I shift her gently into the seat next to me, keeping her hand in mine. The warmth gives me strength while my body cools.

My eyes are on our connected fingers. I rub a thumb over her palm. "I have to tell you something important." I take a deep breath and release it. Then I meet her eyes.

"There's only one other person in the world who knows what I'm about to tell you."

Her hand squeezes mine. Her eyes are concerned, maybe a little insecure, but underneath there's a steady warmth. "You're safe with me."

I search her face for a moment. "You know how I told you about my mom dying?"

She nods, but her eyes turn wary. "Yeah."

I take another fortifying breath and release it. "She had a heart condition. It's called hypertrophic cardiomyopathy. It's where the muscle between the heart chambers thickens. In normal people, it's not necessarily a problem . . . but there is this other thing called athlete's heart. The heart is a muscle and when it's worked out a lot, just like any other muscle, it gets thicker. A more serious problem can happen when both conditions coincide—it exacerbates the thickening of the lining in the heart and blocks blood flow."

She blinks and her hand tightens on mine. "What are you saying?"

I swallow past the lump in my throat. "It started with chest pains, but only during major exertion. Most of the time, it was minor things. Shortness of breath. Dizziness. But I didn't go to the team doctors. I already knew, even then."

"Knew what?"

"I have the same thing that killed my mom. It's genetic."

The ensuing silence is heavy, but I could almost float away, I feel so light. Those words have burdened me for months. Their release is a relief, but with relief comes clarity.

This is really happening to me.

"Are you trying to tell me you're dying?"

"No. Not . . . necessarily."

"Can they fix it?" Her voice rises at the end.

"There are some options. They want me to have surgery."

"When?"

"I . . . I don't know."

Her head is shaking, her shoulders rigid. "Why wouldn't you know?"

"It's not that simple. Heart surgery at this point is career suicide."

"Brent. You can't put football ahead of existing." She pulls her hand out of mine. "Corpses don't get touchdowns."

My hands feel empty without her fingers in mine. "Well, when you put it that way."

"I'm not kidding." And for the first time, she really isn't. Her mouth is turned down, and her eyes are already filling with tears. I've never seen her like this. I've seen her goofy and feisty and scared and happy, but never like this. She looks broken.

"There's no guarantee I'm going to die. And I have other options. There's some kind of implant. It would restart my heart in case it stopped. Why are you so upset?"

"You just told me you're dying and you're not doing anything to fix it. How long have you known?"

"Since before last season."

"You've known for a year, and you've done nothing?" I open my mouth to answer, but then her eyes lift and she says, "You played all last season. What if you had dropped dead on the field? That happens to athletes! I've heard of it."

"I didn't die." Although I've always known that I could. I just didn't think about it too hard. Never allowed myself to sit inside the possibility and truly consider it.

"But you could have. You still could."

"Maybe. But we could all die at any moment. There are a lot of what-ifs."

And we're getting off track. There was a reason I brought all this up. I have to tell her about my broken cock. But she's so agitated, words just pile up in my throat.

She stands and starts pacing the ground in front of me. "Brent, you have to have this surgery."

"I've been weighing my options with my doctor."

A frustrated sound leaves her mouth. "I can't believe they let you play." Her hands are wringing.

"They didn't let me do anything, B. I told you, no one knows about my condition. Except my doctor and you."

"Why would you not tell anyone?"

How *could* I tell anyone? "I . . . was in denial. I didn't want to believe it and then I couldn't risk it getting out. Football is my life." Doesn't she understand that?

"How is football more important than your actual life?"

"It's all I have. It's what I live for. It's what I've always done, since I was five. It's my happy place. After Mom died . . . nothing else in my life has ever been consistent except Marc, and he has his own life. If I can't play, I—" I don't know how to explain it. "Nothing would be worth it."

Her head swivels back and forth. "Unbelievable. You're just like your father. Maybe you need something else worth living for," she snaps and then stills. With a heavy swallow, she steps back from me. "I have to go."

"You're leaving? Now?" I glance over at the clock. It's nearly eleven.

"I have to go," she says again.

"I thought you would understand. You're my . . . friend. More than a friend. You're supposed to support me."

"And you're supposed to stick around." Her voice is soft and full of tears.

140

Another step back and she turns and walks out. She doesn't slam the door. I barely hear the soft click as she shuts it gently behind her.

I'm too mad at her and myself to do anything but stare at the wall and take deep breaths. I need to stay calm. My heart races in my chest like a ticking time bomb.

She was so hurt . . . because I might die. Because she might lose me. She really cares. For me. Not my name or my money or my position on the field.

And I care about her.

And she's gone . . . where exactly?

I pick up my cell phone and send her a text. Screw playing it cool. Maybe it's needy or annoying or desperate, I don't care.

I'm so sorry. Please come back.

No response. I pull up the video feed to her apartment and wait, watching until I see her go home, unlock the door, and slip inside.

What if something happens and I'm not there to help?

I know she said they put something over the entrance to the dumbwaiter, but I don't think they've done the concrete pour yet.

Her safety is more important to me than air. I'm worried about her. And she's worried about me.

A bitter laugh escapes my lips. She's right. I am like my father. Nothing is more important than his business. And for me, nothing has mattered more than football.

But there are more important things in life. Family. Marc. Bethany.

My life can be worth something even if I can't play.

I pick up my phone and call but it rings once and then goes to voicemail.

Chapter Sixteen

"This is terrible."
"Keep going."
–Karen Kilgariff and Georgia Hardstark
My Favorite Murder episode 42

Bethany

I'm the worst person in the whole world.

If there were any justice, I would be run over by a cab, then peed on by a homeless person, then run over again and set on fire.

Brent just told me he has a life-threatening condition and what do I do? Run away and avoid his calls.

Because that's a supportive reaction.

I'm well aware of my own abandonment problems. Everyone leaves or disappoints me. My dad, my mom, and every man I've ever slept with or dated or had lukewarm feelings for. And now Brent.

My issues have issues.

And I'm not alone. He runs, too. Avoids problems at all costs.

Hell, running to the other side of the city is nothing for me. I ran to the other side of the *country* to escape my problems. Which are nothing compared to Brent over here, risking his life and denying a serious health issue.

We're quite the pair.

I step off the elevator, wiping my eyes right as Steven and Natalie are getting on.

"Hey, Bethany," Steven says.

"Where are you guys headed so late?" I ask brightly, like infusing my voice with cheer will hide the red meltdown splotched all over my face.

"We're going to Natalie's place. I'm going to stay there tonight because we're leaving in the morning for an out-of-town Frequent Flyer meeting."

Right. The bird cult.

"Sounds like a fun time."

"We'll be back late tomorrow. Will you check on Martha while we're gone?"

"Absolutely. You guys have a great trip."

It isn't until I'm alone with nothing but empty hands and a heart full of regret that I realize I left my overnight bag with my toothbrush and everything back at Brent's place.

Fuck.

I sit on the couch and stare at the blank TV. After ten minutes of moping, I'm angrier at myself than I am at him. He's right. I should support him. I want to support him. But how can I when he's literally risking his life? He's being selfish. Or maybe I'm being selfish. I don't know, and I have no one to talk to about it since I promised I wouldn't tell anyone.

Then I make more bad decisions by turning on my laptop and googling Brent's condition.

Hypertrophic cardiomyopathy.

It takes me a couple tries to figure out the spelling, but then a whole slew of information comes up.

After reading some articles and trying a search that includes both the condition and athlete's heart, I'm about to have a heart attack myself. Now I'm really convinced he's going to die at any second and probably has pulmonary disease, cancer, and diabetes to boot.

Eventually, I shut the computer and try to sleep.

I can't.

I shouldn't have run out on Brent, but I panicked. I don't think I can handle anything bad happening to him. But I'm already too close. And it's not like I can escape him — we have the charity game in a couple days and I know I'll see him then. I work for his dad, so I might even see him around the office.

I'm an idiot. I can't hide from him. I don't want to hide from him.

I'm still lying there, mentally berating myself when I hear it.

Thump. Thump. Thump.

Maybe it's just neighbors stomping around upstairs. That happens, right? I mean, orgies happen upstairs.

Thumpthumpthump.

It's not coming from above this time. It's coming from the closet.

The cabinet in the hallway I've been using as a dresser is made of thick oak. It's hard to push, but it's good obstructive material. I shift and push with my arms and legs until it's blocking the door to the closet and the only sounds left are my own pants.

I haven't heard any noises since I started pushing the dresser. I stand in silence, catching my breath. Everything is quiet.

Bang!

The sound is right on the door, as if someone in the closet used their fist to pound on the wood.

Fuck!

I run out to the living room, and grab my phone.

I push 9 and then stop.

Wait.

I can't call the cops. They've already been here and think I'm a nut job. By the time they arrive, the closet will be empty and I'll get the fruitcake looks again.

Shit.

What to do?

I exit my apartment, locking the door behind me. Should I Uber it to work? I can't spend the money.

Maybe . . .

I knock on Martha's door. The TV is loud. A up-tempo music thumps through the door, along with the echo of rhythmic counting. Is she watching an exercise video?

I'm about to run away — why is she watching TV on full blast? — when she opens the door in her nightgown and curlers.

"So I know that Steven is gone . . . mind if I steal his bed for the night?"

~*~

The ringing phone jolts me from sleep. I swear I just shut my eyes two minutes ago.

Martha was up all night blasting 1980s aerobicize videos. When I asked her about it, she said she enjoys the music. Listening to the shouts of overly excited fitness gurus all night is better than thumps or bangs or potential murderers, I guess, so there's that.

I pull my cell from the table next to Steven's bed and answer without checking the number.

"Hello?"

"It's me. Don't hang up."

Mom.

Before I have a chance to say anything, she's talking. Her words are clear, but her voice is unsteady all the same. It's not the slurred words that mean she's been hitting the bottle. It's the shaky, anxious tones of detox. "I'm sorry. I know there's nothing I can say that will make it better, but I promise I'm going to try. I haven't drunk anything in two days."

"That's good, Mom." But can I trust it? She sounds sober now, but we've been here before and it never lasts long.

"I'm looking into some places I can get help. My insurance doesn't cover a lot, so I'll have to finance part of it. And you don't owe me anything and I know I don't deserve it, but I need a cosigner. I'll pay you back."

I take a breath and think. Now this, this is different. She's never apologized or offered to pay me back for anything. And I've been covering a lot of her expenses over the years.

Although I'm not sure if I can trust this sudden change, I can't say no. What if this is the time she turns it all around?

"Send me information on the program you want to join. I'll think about it."

She's crying. Quietly, but the hitch in her breath gives her away. "I've really messed up."

"You have. But you can make it better."

We talk for a few more minutes until I realize I'm late for work and I have to hang up.

Most of the time, Mr. Crawford comes in late anyway, but I have to take three trains to get to Park Avenue and if I'm not there when he is, I'm fucked.

There are alerts on my phone—more Google alerts about Mr. Crawford. I don't have a chance to check them until I'm on the crowded train, hanging on to a pole with one hand, hair still wet but mostly put together.

Once again the news isn't really about Mr. Crawford, but Brent.

And me.

Oh fuck.

Even with the Oakland hat on, someone recognized him. Should have expected that. I mean, he's like 220 pounds of brawny man meat. You can't cover that body up with a hat and sunglasses.

The headline screams, *Brent Crawford and the Other Woman!* Below are pictures of us kissing on the Staten Island Ferry. Another one of Brent smiling down at me while I shove a hot dog in my face. Yet another one on the subway. I'm sitting in his lap and talking so my eyes are partially closed and my mouth is half open and Brent is laughing and looking amazing while I appear deranged.

Lovely.

There are highlights about his dinner with Angela Sinclair and their fathers from the other week, hence the alert. Then right after that, pictures of Angela Sinclair with large sunglasses, hiding from paparazzi.

A woman scorned, it reads.

"She's a lesbian!" I yell at my phone.

"Who cares!" another commuter yells from somewhere on the train.

"Exactly!" I yell back.

My heart hurts looking at all the pictures. Not only because I look terrible in every one. Not even because the comments below the articles are slamming me for being an old dinosaur skank, although that hurts a little, but they're also a reminder of what I'm going to lose.

Brent.

With a groan I think about his reaction to all this. I'm sure his father and publicist are going to love these newsflashes.

Three hours later and I'm ready to curl up into a ball and die.

Work sucks.

I'm exhausted.

I call the super and he insists they covered the dumbwaiter. When I tell him there are still weird noises, he says he'll look into it sometime today.

On my first break, I slip into the bathroom and call Freya. She's been blowing up my phone all morning.

"You were supposed to move to New York and not be a skank. What happened?"

I laugh because what else can I do? "I'm not being a skank. Brent and I haven't done anything other than kiss." And have a super-hot make-out session, which he then stopped to tell me he's freaking dying, but I can't really mention that bit. "And he never dated Angela Sinclair. It's all bullshit."

"But you're together? Like, *together*. With Brent Crawford? Dude."

"I don't think it's like that. We had a fight."

"About what? The pictures? Angela Sinclair? Did she show up at your apartment with her perfectly groomed eyebrows and tell you to lay off her man with no expression whatsoever because the Botox has frozen her face?"

"Not quite." I can't tell Freya that Angela bats for the other team. That would be royally messed up.

"Tell me what's going on!"

"It's . . . complicated. I'll call you later and tell you everything." Almost everything. "I'm at work now and I can't really talk."

"You better call me tonight or I will fly out there and tell everyone we're lesbian lovers and Brent is actually the other woman."

I laugh. Oh the irony. Freya always has a way of making me feel better.

When I get back to my desk, Mr. Crawford is waiting, standing in the office door, glowering at me as I approach.

And all my good feelings disappear in a puff of stress and anxiety.

"Where were you?"

"I was taking a break."

"I need you to confirm the meeting this afternoon."

"I confirmed it two days ago, Mr. Crawford, and again this morning."

"Do it again."

I take a deep breath and count to ten. "Of course, Mr. Crawford," I say in the sickliest, sweetest voice I can muster.

He's onto me. He's glaring as I walk by him and primly sit at my desk.

"Was there anything else, sir?"

"Brent's coming for the meeting." He points a finger at me. "Don't flirt with him."

"I would never behave in an unprofessional manner in the workplace, sir."

"Maybe not but I hear you're acting less than professional outside work. I have plans for Brent and they don't involve a social climber. Trying to sleep with the boss's son won't get you anything but screwed. In more ways than one."

My mouth falls open.

He has got to be kidding me.

"I know you need this job," he continues. "If you stay away from Brent, I'll let you keep it. If you don't . . . well, I have a lot of connections in this city, and when I'm done, you won't be able to keep a roof over your alcoholic mother's head."

The words are emotionless. His face is as hard and blank as granite.

He's done research on me. On my family? How does he know about Mom? What is he, the mob?

My eyes are stinging.

As Mr. Crawford slinks back into his office, I sink in my seat but keep my head high, gazing up at the ceiling and hoping gravity will prevent my next breakdown. I will not lose it. I will not give him the satisfaction.

My mind is whirring with his threats. Even if I wanted to keep Brent, I can't.

I open the drawer where Marc left another note for me.

When work feels overwhelming, remember that you're going to die.

The irony piles up around here like snow on Everest.

A few seconds later, Mr. Crawford is back at my desk. I force myself to meet his eyes. I set my jaw, ready for more.

"Don't tell Brent about this conversation." He waves an irritated hand at me and sets off again, this time in the direction of Marc's office down the hall.

I slump back, all my bravado flying straight out the window. I need a nap. Or a good cry. My eyes burn with exhaustion and exasperation.

I should quit. Or sue. Or, at the very least, stop protecting Mr. Crawford from someone else suing.

No. I'm not doing any of that. I need this job. I can't afford a lawyer. And I have too much work ethic to be a crappy employee.

I swallow back my emotions. I will not cry. I hate it when I get emotional; my face turns into a blotchy mess.

Taking deep breaths, I focus on the positive: I am smart. I can do this. I have a nice butt and killer boobs, despite what those commenters were saying online.

I'm not a home-wrecking skankalopagus.

I didn't get fired.

Yet.

These are all good things.

I try to get back to work but I keep having to blink away tears and I can't focus on the spreadsheets in front of me.

Even the spreadsheets!

Screw Mr. Crawford and all his bull-fuckery and fake tan and piles of money.

Down the hall, the elevator dings and I catch a glimpse of Brent's tall form emerging as the doors slide open. Dammit. I don't want him to see me like this.

Pretending my body is suddenly rubber, I slump and slither like a boneless snake down under the desk. From my vantage as a puddle on the floor, his athletic shoes approach.

His head pops around my chair.

Apparently, my not-so-quick thinking didn't fool him.

His brows lift and his mouth twitches.

"I dropped my contact," I say.

The twitching lips turn into a full-out grin. Damn him and his dimples.

"You don't wear contacts."

"I know." Sigh.

He steps back and I very awkwardly propel myself out from my hiding spot. Brent lends a hand, pulling me up, his fingers strong and warm.

His eyes search mine. "Hi." He's still holding my hand. "I brought your stuff."

He has my pink bag flung over his shoulder.

Of course he brought my bag. He's considerate. Unlike me, the girl who he spilled his heart to — literally — and ran away screaming.

And now I'll have to keep running to keep my job.

The thought makes the tears well again.

"I'm sorry."

"I'm sorry, too." The tears make a final push and spill over. I try to blink the dampness away but it doesn't help when they're running down my cheeks, the traitorous drops of emotion.

He pulls me into him, strong arms wrapping around my body and enveloping me in comforting warmth. This must be the safest and best-smelling place in the whole world.

But what if Mr. Crawford comes back and sees?

"Are you sniffing me?"

"My nose is running. I'm just trying to not get my boogers all over you."

"I would believe that if you weren't literally lifting my sleeve from my arm to smell it."

I step back, glancing around to make sure no one saw before meeting his eyes.

He always looks a bit worn out and tired—and now I know the reason why—but today the grey smudges are even darker, the lines around his eyes deeper.

"Are we okay?" His deep blue gaze searches mine.

I nod. "Yes. I just don't want you to . . ." One hand comes up in futility.

"I know. I get it. I was so worried about you, watching the cameras all night. You left at one point and I thought maybe you were coming back to my place."

I shouldn't tell him. But I can't lie, not ever, but especially not when he's gazing at me with penetrating, blue-eyed concern. "There were some sounds. I stayed with Martha."

His gaze lasers in on me. "You said yesterday the super covered the dumbwaiter entrance. There were still noises?"

I nod once.

"Will you come home tonight?"

Home, he says. Like his apartment is ours. I bite my lip. "I already called the super this morning. They're going to double-check it. I'll be fine at my place."

"I'm still worried about you. Why is someone breaking in there to begin with?"

I shrug. "No clue. But it's got to stop now. There's no other entrance. Besides, did you see the news?"

"What news?"

"There were photos of us together, online."

He grimaces. "I try not to look at press stuff. But I did have a few missed calls from Roger this morning."

"It's probably better if I stay away for a couple days so you aren't in the limelight. They had some pictures of Angela all upset. I know she's not, but it's bad press."

His lips turn down. "I don't care about bad press."

Your dad does, and I need to keep my job.

But I keep those thoughts to myself.

His eyes are dark and his brows are lowered. There's a stagnant pause and it feels an awful lot like we're breaking up.

Were we ever really together to begin with?

"I'll still see you at the game Saturday?" he asks.

"Yeah. Of course." I force a smile but it stretches my face like a grimace.

He opens his mouth and then shuts it again.

"Brent." Mr. Crawford is back. He won't meet my eyes. "You ready to go?"

I sit down, turning my chair so my back is to both of them.

"Yeah." Brent pauses. I sense his gaze on the back of my neck like a caress. I don't turn around. "I'm ready."

They walk down the hall, Mr. Crawford jabbering about their client meeting and blah blah blah. I focus on my inbox and do my best to ignore the sound of Brent walking away.

Chapter Seventeen

If it is easy, then you are doing it wrong.
–Gabby Williams

Brent

The charity baseball game is always a blast. I love working with the kids, seeing their eyes light up when they make a home run or hit a ball or steal a base. The crowd is always big—everyone wants to see the celebrities on the field—and it's great to make money for a good cause.

Outwardly, I help the kids and cheer and play. Inwardly, anxiety builds.

I need to talk to Bethany.

I miss her.

The last two days have been like a hellish trip into the past—like the sun is blocked out and the world is drowning in gloom. Just like it was before Bethany. I move from one day to the next, going through the motions without really feeling anything.

One of the kids hits the ball between second and third base, sending it bumping into the outfield, and the crowd goes wild. I run alongside him to first, yelling encouragement. We high five when he lands on the plate.

I'm grinning, but at the same time I can't wait for the game to be over.

Dad hasn't been helping my depression. He makes comments about Bethany, about the pictures of us. He doesn't say it outright, but it's clear he doesn't want me to see her. He mentioned Angela again and I shut him down.

I managed to put Roger off for another week, but I won't be able to wait much longer. Not without a valid reason. He tells me to ignore the press about Bethany. Everything is always *no comment*. My personal life is my personal life.

I'm going to have to tell him the truth.

Angela doesn't mind the press, either. In fact, she sounds downright chipper when we talk. She can't tell her dad about Charlie.

I'm basically her beard.

My cardiologist called to badger me again, but this time I agreed to the surgery. I have to, or nothing will ever change. I choose life, even if it's not with Bethany, but I hope it is.

My mind circles back to her constantly. I miss the crazy things that pop out of her mouth at the most unexpected times. I miss the facial expressions that convey every possible thought in her head. I miss the way she makes me laugh and forget all my troubles. Her presence has become a soothing balm, a comfort, and now that she's gone it's like I'm missing my best friend.

I don't know how many minutes I have left, and I don't want to miss any I could be spending with her.

Once the game is over, I have to sign autographs, pose for pictures, and shake hands with sponsors and fans. It all takes forever and by the time most of the people have cleared out, I'm worried she's already gone.

But she's not. She had things to deal with after the game, too, since she helped to set up most of it.

I find her at Scarlett's truck in the parking lot, helping her pack up the tables and chairs set up outside the mobile dessert shop.

She turns as I approach. When she sees me her face brightens, but then she glances to the side and bites her lip. She's in jeans and a plain T-shirt. There's a ball cap on her head and a smudge of dirt on her cheek.

She's everything I didn't know I needed.

"Hey," she says.

I don't waste any time. "Can I take you to dinner?"

Scarlett clears her throat from the window of the truck where she was wiping down the counter. "I'll see you later, Bethany. Nice to see you Brent, great game."

"Thanks, Scarlett."

She shuts the window to give us a semblance of privacy.

"So. Dinner?" I try again.

She hesitates.

"Please, B? I've really missed you."

Her lips tilt up and she finally meets my eyes. "I've missed you, too."

"Really? How much?"

She rolls her eyes. "Don't push it, buddy. I'll go to dinner with you, but I don't want any paparazzi to see us."

"I know. I've already heard it from Dad, but it will be nothing like that, I promise. We're actually going to get some food on the go. We won't even get out of the car. I have a few places to add to our tour from the other day."

I can see the indecision warring in her eyes. She glances around, as if she's afraid a paparazzo will pop out of the bushes, but finally she relents.

"Okay."

Thirty minutes later, we're eating burritos in the Panamera.

"I'm going to get beans and rice all over your beautiful car."

I shrug. "I'll get it cleaned."

"So what's this tour all about? Famous hotels of New York?" She motions to the giant red hotel to our right.

I've parked right outside Hotel Chelsea.

"This, my friend, is where Sid Vicious murdered Nancy Spungen. Allegedly."

Her mouth pops open in surprise and then she laughs. A good laugh, head back, throat exposed. The sight makes me grin. It's nice to make her laugh like she does for me.

She puts a hand to her chest. "You brought me to the scene of a horrible crime. You really must like me."

I laugh with her. "I really know how to show a lady a nice time."

"Sid Vicious was the Sex Pistols guy, right?" she asks before taking a bite of her food.

"Yep. He died before they could try him for the murder—overdose. They were both heavy into drugs so there are lots of theories about her death. If it wasn't Sid, it could have been a drug dealer, or some people think it might have been an accident since they were both strung out."

She frowns and glances down at her lap. "How sad."

"But wait." I pull out of the parking spot into traffic. "It gets so much worse."

We drive down Tenth Avenue and then take West Forty-Seventh over to Twelfth.

"The Hudson River," I say as we drive next to the churning waters. "The unfortunate location of many a dead-body drop-off. Spring is a good time for finding remains since the warming of the waters causes the corpses to rise."

"So creepy."

"Seriously though."

Ten minutes later, we pull up outside of a large soccer field, part of Riverside Park off Henry Hudson Parkway. On our other side, the Hudson River is an inky black streak in the darkness.

"Who died here?"

"This is where Lucien Carr killed David Kammerer."

"Oh, I know this one! Lucien was friends with Jack Kerouac. The beatnik dudes."

"You know your murders."

"You're damn right I do."

We continue our drive through Central Park, the bare branches above us reaching toward the dark sky like skeleton arms glinting in the glare from headlights and street lamps. "Yet another place there are too many murders to mention." And end up at Dorrian's Red Hand.

"Ah the preppy murder. Such a bunch of bullshit. I can't believe that guy pretty much got away with murder."

"And set the tone for assault against women for years to come."

"Right? Let's put the victim on the stand. She was wearing a short dress, you know, so clearly she was asking to be murdered." Her words are jokey, like normal, but the tone is flat. Subdued. Like a chandelier with half the bulbs burnt out. Is that my fault?

I keep my own tone light. "Even more ironically, the Red Hand refers to an old Gaelic legend involving murder."

Her brows lift. "No way."

"Way."

She smiles, the motion soft and brief.

There's a pause while we gaze at the red-canopied restaurant and then she yawns.

"I should take you home."

She nods. "I am pretty beat. It was a busy day."

158

"You did a great job with the game. Thank you for everything."

"You're welcome."

We drive in silence the ten minutes it takes to get back to her apartment.

I want to tell her the truth. About everything. She deserves to know the real reason I pulled away the other night. I can't leave it like this.

But the words stick in my throat. I should just let her go.

She hesitates before getting out of the car, hand on the door. "Do you want to come up? I . . . want to talk to you. And I'm not gonna lie, I don't really want to be alone."

"I'll come up." Thank God.

Once we're upstairs sitting on her futon—which is still in the bed position, blankets strewn everywhere—I take her hand, linking her fingers in mine.

She speaks first. "I'm sorry I freaked. I don't want you to drop dead."

"No, I'm glad you did."

Her answering smile is wry. "You're glad I acted like a weirdo and bolted on you?"

"Kind of. I mean, I'm used to two scenarios: women who throw themselves at me because of my fame and position, or women who don't like me at all for the same reasons. You don't care about money or fame, but you're worried about me as a person and friend. That you care enough to get mad at me actually means a lot."

"Well then. I'll try to get pissed off at you more often." Her fingers squeeze mine.

I blow out a relieved breath. "I'll try to deserve it. But you were right to be pissed. I've been ignoring my problems for too long and it doesn't make them go away."

159

"I totally understand. Sometimes it's easier to escape than to face things head on. We all have our crutch."

And I have one more secret to tell her. For some reason, this is harder to reveal than the potentially fatal one.

"There's something else I need to tell you."

She groans. "There's more? Diabetes? Pulmonary disease?"

"What? No, nothing like that. Only the one life-threatening condition. Which I am going to have surgery for. It's pending scheduling. I have to tell you though . . . when I pulled away the other night, it wasn't just because of my heart condition." I stop, take a deep breath. "I have to take these pills, beta-blockers. They help with the chest pains and everything. They aren't foolproof, but they help. The thing is . . . there are side effects."

"Side effects?"

I glance away, not wanting to see her response. "One of the side effects is impotence."

Her hand is still in mine, not moving. Waiting for her reaction is killing me, even though only seconds have passed. I finally meet her eyes.

She blinks at me. "You mean . . . ?"

"Yeah."

She releases a long, relieved breath. "Oh thank God."

A startled laugh escapes me. Only Bethany would respond in the complete opposite way of what I expected. No disgust, horror, or pity. Relief is a welcome surprise. "That makes you happy?"

"I just, I really thought you weren't attracted to me like, at all. I mean, the times we've woken up together there wasn't even morning wood sticking me in the back. All this time, I figured you just weren't into me. Which is why the kissing and stuff was real confusing. Then I thought maybe you were forcing it but it wasn't really there."

"No. The opposite is true. It's weird because even though I can't really . . ."

"Get hard?"

"Yes, that." I give in to the urge to brush a wayward curl out of her face, rubbing the silky strand with my fingers before releasing it. "I am still very much attracted to you. The pills don't affect my libido. I still feel passion and lust and want. But I can't do much about it."

"Dude. That sucks."

"Tell me about it."

She bites her lip and there's a curious gleam in her eyes that I recognize.

"Go ahead." I shake my head with a laugh as she scoots closer and her hand tightens around mine.

"Have you tried to, you know, get it on with anyone since the heart thing? I mean, besides the other night, when it was just about me."

"No. I mean, it's not like I have time to fool around with people during the season and whatnot and I was already pretty messed up from Bella. And then with Gwen—"

"Wait, does she know?"

"She knows about the impotence. She doesn't know about the heart condition. The only way I could get her to agree to the fake relationship was to tell her the truth. About that part, anyway. The doctor said impotence is a fairly common side effect, and it's not permanent. It gets better when I stop taking the blockers, but then the side effects from the HCM get worse."

She winces. "Ugh. So even if you, like, rub it and stuff, nothing happens?"

"Not really. Sometimes it will get a little harder, but it doesn't last long and it doesn't relieve anything." I shift a little and rub a damp palm against the thigh of my pants.

"What about a little blue pill?"

I shake my head. "Nope. I didn't try it, because of the heart condition. I can't take anything like that without further risk. Besides, I did some research early on and I guess forcing an erection isn't satisfying. It's like going through the motions but not experiencing the pleasure, you know?"

She shakes her head. "No idea. I wish I had a penis sometimes. Even if you can't get it up, you can still pee standing up so there's that."

Laughter bubbles out of me, a mixture of humor and relief. I can't believe she's making me laugh about even this. "True."

"So after you have the surgery and stop taking the blockers, then your penis will come back from the dead?"

I rub my head with a chuckle. Of all the conversations I pictured us having about this, it didn't quite go like this. "Yes, once I stop taking the beta-blockers, it should be business as usual."

"Awesome. And when are you having the surgery?"

"Want to mark your calendar?"

"Hell yeah I do." She grins but then her smile falters and she looks down at our joined hands. "That is, if you still want me at that point."

"Bethany. I will always want you." I tuck a finger under her chin to bring her gaze to mine and then I kiss her.

It's different from before. Before there were unsaid things between us, my ever-present problems that always lingered in the back of my mind, keeping me from being truly present.

Now there's nothing between us. She knows everything. And she's still here and she doesn't give a shit.

She's amazing.

I deepen the kiss, angling her head back, and she turns into putty in my arms. She leans into me, her head

162

tilting and her body melting into mine, the heat of her breasts against my chest making me groan.

She pulls back for a moment. "If this makes you uncomfortable, we don't have to."

I cup her face in my hands. "I want to. You have no idea how badly. The other night, when you fell apart in my arms, was . . . indescribable."

Her cheeks flush. "I thought so, too, but—"

"No buts." I kiss the pink glow along her jaw, trailing my lips to just behind her ear, and I'm rewarded with an answering shudder.

This isn't like the last time, no frantic movements and rushing heat. I want her to know exactly how much I treasure her.

Cupping her face in my hands, I pepper her lips with soft nibbles, patient and languorous, determined to keep the moment slow and sweet.

Even when her hands tug at my hair and her mouth opens, I continue to taste her with careful dips and strokes.

"Brent." Her voice is breathy and aroused and my stomach quivers in response.

Leaning back, I remove her shirt, taking the time to graze the soft skin of her arms and sides with my fingers as the fabric slips up and over her head.

She reaches for me, fiddling with the bottom of my shirt.

I help her tug the clothes over my head and then have the satisfaction of watching her eyes glaze over as she runs a hungry gaze down my chest. Her hands are fisted at her side and I grab one and bring it to my skin.

"You can touch me." The words are a whisper in the dark.

And she does, running careful fingers over abs, up to my chest, lingering over my pecs and grazing my nipples until I can't take it anymore.

I kneel at her feet to remove her shoes, stopping to kiss her insoles and ankles, marveling at the softness of her skin and the hitch in her breath every time I trace her flesh.

Reaching up, I tug at her pants until she's sitting in front of me in nothing but a bra and underwear.

"You're more amazing than anything I've dreamed."

"Brent," she says again, until I begin kissing my way up the inside of her leg and then her head falls back on a moan.

"Bethany," I say and her head comes up. "Look at me." I move up her body further, turning kisses into torturous sucks and grazes of teeth along her inner thigh, my eyes never leaving hers. Her gaze turns dark and drowsy as her legs fall open and I near her panties, already damp with arousal.

With a slow, languid gesture I rub her through the fabric with one gentle finger.

She moans, eyes falling shut again. I wish I could swallow the sound.

Lust surges inside me, seeking release that can only be spent through her. Taking a deep breath, I inhale her wildflower scent mixed with the spice of arousal that does nothing to calm the inflamed need licking through my body. I tug the strip of fabric between her legs to the side and press my mouth against her heat.

My reward is a strangled groan, louder than the last. She arches back and I wrap my arms around her thighs to hold her in place.

I start with gentle kisses mixed with furtive licks, as slow and soothing as I can manage just to savor her as long as possible, learning what she likes, what makes her crazy, what makes her squirm and buck and pant.

It's not enough. I drag her panties down and off, needing to get closer to everything. And it is everything. Her body, her sounds, her smell. She's the rush of the

164

crowd roaring when I'm running onto the field. The touchdown pass that hits me right in the chest as I'm crossing the line into the end zone. The championship win, the Super Bowl ring.

I pull her to the edge of the futon, lifting one trim leg up onto my bare shoulder. Her calves are smooth and strong, flexing against my skin. I force myself to slow down, then speed up, then slow again, teasing her, tormenting her. Her leg trembles against me.

Her hips start to shudder, her hands reaching into my hair.

"Brent," she pants. "Please."

I increase the intensity. Tongue thrusting and plundering until the surge moves through her like a tsunami.

She shakes with the intensity, shattering with my name on her lips and her thighs clenching around my head.

When her movements finally subside and she relaxes back, formerly tense muscles now limp, I plant a few more kisses on her thighs and climb over to meet her on the bed.

She immediately curls into me. "Brent." My name is a puff warm of air against my skin. "That was . . . everything."

"Not quite everything."

She laughs. "Almost everything. Close enough. I feel terrible."

I trail a finger over her smooth shoulder and she shivers. "That's not exactly what I hoped to hear."

"You know what I mean. I feel great. But also terrible that I can't reciprocate."

"Don't feel bad. I don't. That was amazing. To watch you fall apart because of me? That's the next best thing."

165

"Well. When your surgery thing is all done, I'm going to rock your world about fourteen million times to make up for it."

"Fourteen million? Not Fifteen?"

"Fine, fifteen million. Sheesh you're needy."

Her laugh is low and soft and sends tingles through my body. I want to make her laugh every day.

~*~

We lay in silence for a few minutes, absorbing the feel of each other's bodies, memorizing scents and listening to gentle breaths.

After a time, she pulls her head up to meet my eyes. "There's something I need to tell you. Part of the real reason I freaked and ran. You know how I told you my mom is a level ten clinger? She wasn't always that way. Remember when I told you my dad died from poisoning?"

"Yes." It strikes me now how vague she was about it before. How she always changed the subject. Is she going to open up now? Does this mean she trusts me?

"Unintentional poisoning is a formal way to describe an accidental overdose. It's what I use because I don't want to deal with the truth."

I hold her a little tighter. "I'm so sorry."

She shakes her head at my apology. "That's not even the worst part. After he died, Mom kind of lost her shit. I mean, she really couldn't handle it. I think she felt guilty about how he died, like she should have been able to fix him or something. She started drinking to escape her guilt and then it got progressively worse. She lost her job.

166

I had to pay for everything. She would get mean sometimes, call me names."

I wince and rub her arm. She recites the words like they don't matter, but it has to hurt. No one wants to feel unloved by a parent. I understand that pain. "Like what?"

"You know, a dirty whore, useless daughter. Things like that."

"It's not true."

"Oh, I know that." Her words are light, but her eyes dart away from mine. "She didn't mean it. It was the booze talking. She never remembered saying it the next day. But it made it hard to be around her. Which is why I would go out and then stay the night with other people."

"Like friends?"

"Not really." She sighs. "So the truth is that I let all my friends think I was stuck in the old college glory days, partying all the time and hooking up with randoms. I would rather they think I was sleeping around than tell them the truth—that I didn't want to go home. Although, admittedly, sometimes it *was* because I was horny. Just not as much as I let my friends believe. Do you think I'm a weirdo?" She tilts her head away, hiding her eyes from view.

I cup her face, tilting her back to meet my eyes. "B, no. No way. You're human. You were coping with a lot of shit. I would never hold any of that against you. You're allowed to do what you want with your life. Whatever makes you happy. You were in a bad situation and you got away and never stopped helping your mom. A lot of people wouldn't have the strength to cope and grow like you have." I tug her closer.

"There's more."

I wait while she pulls her thoughts together.

"Last week she completely cleared out my bank accounts."

My hand stops moving on her arm. "Holy shit. Why didn't you tell me?"

"It's not your responsibility."

"I know, but I can help you. How did she manage that?"

She closes her eyes and shakes her head. "It's my fault. I should have known better. I had her name on my accounts for emergencies. Apparently needing vodka is now an emergency."

"If you need money, I can—"

She meets my gaze and puts a stalling hand on my arm. "No. No, Brent, I don't need money. I got her name removed and I cut her off. This all happened last week. Then she called me the other morning and she said she's going to rehab. It's a good thing. It's making her face her demons. Hopefully it will stick."

I don't push the issue. I want to, but I know she won't take it. It's one of the things I love about her. "I hope so, too. You're a strong, smart woman." Who will hopefully come to me for help if she needs it.

"Thanks." Her answering smile is subdued. I want to make her laugh.

"Also you have a nice ass."

That startles a chuckle from her. "I like to think so. You're not too shabby yourself." She squeezes one of my biceps.

"Oh yeah? Not too shabby, huh?" I run a finger down her ribs, making her squirm and giggle and I have to kiss her, capture the sound with my lips.

There's a creaking noise and a muffled thunk, and she tenses in my arms.

"It sounds like it's out in the hall. Maybe the neighbor." I kiss her shoulder. "Let me check." I get up to peek out the front door.

"Huh. Nobody out here after all."

"Really? You sure? It sounded awfully close."

I chuckle and slide back under the covers to wrap around her. "Maybe it was just a rat. You know we grow them extra big here."

She shudders in my arms. "Ugh. I guess that's better than a vengeful ghost, but still, I'm glad you're here."

My arms tighten around her and I breathe in deeply, absorbing her wildflower scent. "I'm glad I'm here, too."

Chapter Eighteen

It doesn't matter what your background is and where you come from, if you have dreams and goals, that's all that matters.
–Serena Williams

Bethany

Sunlight wakes me. I blink my eyes open to find Brent lying on his side, facing me.

"Are you watching me sleep?" My voice is thick and drowsy.

"Maybe."

"Creep." I yawn.

"Yep."

"I bet I can be creepier."

"I always sleep better with you for some reason."

"Okay, you win, creeper."

He laughs. "That's not creepy. It's true. You're like a drug."

I smile into my pillow, suddenly shy, then turn my face back to watch him.

"Okay creep-face. Staring contest. Go."

We lay side by side, eyes locked. This will be the easiest bet ever. I could stare at him all day since I'm shocked into stillness by the fact that this gorgeous hunk of a man chose me. His eyes are bright and happy this morning. I trail my gaze over his chiseled jaw and high cheekbones tempered by thin laugh lines and a sensual curve at his lips.

Old remnants of insecurities flare.

He can't mean to stick around. It's all a fluke, brought on by his own self-doubt.

And even if he does, what if something happens to him before surgery? Or during?

What if Mr. Crawford finds out and fires me?

I shove the thoughts down, not wanting them to ruin the moment.

The staring gets cut off when he tilts forward and kisses me. Sweet, gentle pecks and sips.

The night was for ghosts and dreams; the morning is for gentle touches and memorizing everything about each other with soft fingertips.

I trail fingers over the piece of his hair that puffs up at the same spot in the back, the ticklish inside of his elbow, the curve of his bicep. And he explores my landscape, kissing the freckle on my side, tracing the shape of my knee with a finger. All while talking about any odd thing that pops into our heads and laughing for no reason, just for the joy of the moment.

"You're the only person I've slept with more than once," I say when he pulls back slightly.

His smile is everything. "Did we just become best friends?"

"Yup. Will you sing with me at the Catalina Wine Mixer?"

He laughs. "Anytime. Go out with me tonight."

"What are we doing?"

"I want to take you somewhere nice."

"Erm. Somewhere paparazzi won't see us?"

He shrugs. "Can't guarantee anything but I'll do my best. I want to spend time with you. I want everyone to know you're mine."

I scoff. "You're such a romantic."

"With you, yeah."

My stomach flips, like giant butterfly bats flying around and wreaking havoc with my soul.

It would be so easy to fall in love with him.

"So if we go on a really real date . . . does this mean we aren't friends anymore?"

His finger traces my collarbone. "I hope you don't think this is super pathetic since we've only known each other for like a month, but you're my best friend. And I don't see that changing."

"Best friends who make out sometimes."

He grins, his blue eyes bright and happy. "Is there something wrong with that?"

"No." I try to push down the cowlick in the back of his head again and it pops right back up, making me smile. "Are we friends who shower together, too?"

"I think that can be arranged."

~*~

Work sucks. More than usual. Mr. Crawford isn't even here yet and it's a madhouse of people trying to get their lists and to-do items onto my desk so they don't have to deal with him.

Not that I want to deal with him, either. Things are still strained between us since our last blowout.

It gets worse when Charlie emails me a link to an article that hit less than an hour ago.

"Shit."

It's another photo of me with Brent.

It could be worse. We're not making out this time, just eating burritos in his car.

And of course, they caught me with my mouth completely full, chewing, foodstuffs visible in my teeth and Brent has his mouth closed, angled toward me, looking like the model he is.

The universe seriously hates me.

At least there's no reference to Angela in this one, just a note about how we were spotted together eating in his car.

I close the web page and send a fervent prayer to the universe that Mr. Crawford doesn't see it.

There are still a few people at my desk when Mr. Crawford breezes in. Some of them scatter but not quickly enough to avoid overhearing his words.

He slams a paper down on my desk. "You're fired."

Behind him, Stan the security man shuffles his feet, not meeting my eyes.

Blood drains from my face. Dizziness threatens to overwhelm me. This isn't a cute, jokey firing. This is real.

Mr. Crawford's eyes, blue like Brent's, are hard. Cold and calculating.

It's amazing how two people with the same eyes view the world so differently.

My eyes flick to the paper. It's a different article from the one Charlie sent me. This one has pictures of me and Brent arriving at my apartment and an update about him leaving the next morning.

The rest is inferred.

"Security will make sure you pack only your personal belongings and escort you from the building." Without another word he disappears into his office.

As soon as Mr. Crawford's door slams shut, people exit the area—slowly, mind you—totally watching the train wreck the entire time. I don't move.

I can't lose my job.

What about Mom? There's no way I could get her financing now that I'm not gainfully employed.

173

Finally, everyone has pitter-pattered away and I meet Stan's kind eyes.

His face is a study in regret, brows furrowed, lips tilted down.

"It's okay. I don't have much stuff."

"I'm real sorry about this."

"I'll be okay." But the words don't make the ache in my stomach go away.

Twenty minutes later, I'm outside on the sidewalk with a box full of personal items.

At the top of the box, flickering in the crisp breeze, is one last sticky note from Marc.

Never let anyone treat you like a yellow Starburst. You are a pink Starburst.

I don't even smile. I think I'm in shock. Men and women dressed in smart suits with backpacks and briefcases churn around me. They all have somewhere to go. Something important to do.

Three mindless subway stops later, I book it past the bodega to my apartment building.

Everything is numb, like I've been sitting on a block of ice for an hour instead of where I actually am, on the time-worn futon.

Brent left his watch behind on accident and I watch it tick the time. It's a black sports watch with exposed cogs and wheels. TAG Heuer. It probably costs more than a car.

My phone rings and when I pick it up, I realize I have three missed calls.

One is Mom.

One is Brent.

One is Sam.

And Sam's calling again right now.

"Hello?"

"Dude. There might be shit in your walls."

"What? Shit? I don't think I can deal with more bad news right now."

"Not like actual shit, but some kind of treasure!" He's way too excited, the sound a contrast to my own inner turmoil. "Traaay-suurrre!" he yells.

"Are you drunk?"

"Nope. What were you saying about bad news?"

"Nothing. So what's in my walls?"

"Get this. In the 1950s there was this old mob boss dude who was on the run for embezzlement or whatever mob guys run away from, and he hid in your building. While he was on the run. Except it's the apartment next to yours he actually lived in."

He pauses for effect but it goes on way too long. "And?"

"And there are some who think he may have hidden something of serious value in the walls for safekeeping so he could retrieve it when he got out."

"Like what? Drugs?"

"Not drugs, cash money, baby! Or jewels. Or whatever it is Mafia dudes use. Gold bars! Silver coins! Doubloons!"

"This isn't *The Goonies*."

"How do you know?" His tone is offended.

"And you think that's why there have been weird noises and intruders in my apartment? The mob guy's out of prison and seeking his hidden wealth?"

"No, he's dead. But there's this whole website of people who have all these conspiracy theories. With a little digging, anyone could have figured it out. I did. Now I bet there's a bunch of ex-cons teaming up to break in using elaborate methods to steal the goods back."

I snort. "That's ridiculous."

Pause. "Are you okay? You're not being yourself."

"What do you mean?"

"You love ridiculous notions. You're supposed to expand on my heist theory, not knock it down."

"I'm fine." I really don't want to talk about it. "Thanks for the intel, Sam. I'll call you later, okay? Give Gemma my love."

"I will."

I hang up and flop over on the couch. It would be nice if there were riches in my walls. Maybe I could use them for Mom's rehab. And bills. But it's all a pipe dream. If I can't find another job . . . I'm not going to think that way.

Brent will make me feel better. I may have lost my job, but I have him. Even though I don't want to unload my problems all over him. He has enough going on, and I don't want him to feel like he has to help me—in a monetary sense—but maybe he can help me look for a new job.

I try to call him but it goes to voicemail.

I'm sure he's busy.

But a niggling of anxiety won't leave me alone.

Chapter Nineteen

I can fuck up real good.
–Georgia Hardstark
My Favorite Murder episode 124

Brent

I'm doing chores to avoid the inevitable. I pick up a shirt from the floor—the one from yesterday—and smell it. Wildflowers and mint. Bethany is all over it. The scent gives me strength to do what needs to be done.

It takes a bit of deep breathing and tossing my old football around while pacing a hole in the floor, but I finally call the surgeon and schedule the date.

Three weeks.

I have three weeks to tell the world the truth. Well, Dad and Roger, and while they aren't exactly the entire world, they might as well be.

Then the team will have to be informed. Contract rejected.

It's not the money. I have money. It's the dream.

Bethany calls while I'm on the phone and before I can call her back, the phone rings in my hand. It's the front desk.

"There's an Angela Sinclair here to see you, sir," the guard says. "Can we send her up?"

Ever since the last incident with Marissa, they never send anyone up without asking. Unless I've cleared it with them first, like I did with Bethany.

Why is Angela here?

"I'll come down." Not that I think she'll shoot me or anything, but better safe than sorry.

I meet her in the lounge by the guard desk.

"Hey."

She leans in and kisses me on the cheek, grabbing my hands in hers. "Can we talk?"

"Sure." I nod to a couple of chairs and gently extricate my fingers from her grasp. She's being oddly handsy.

She's wearing big dark sunglasses and a beige pea coat over slim white pants and high heels.

"I've been trying to call you," she says once we're sitting.

"Sorry. I've been really busy."

"I understand you want to sow your wild oats now, as they say," she chuckles and removes her glasses, pushing them on top of her blonde head. "But I just want to let you know I'm not going to stand for it when we're married." Her voice is loud, carrying through the lobby.

Even so, the words don't register at first.

Wait. What? Married?

I glance around. Is she delusional?

I search her eyes but her gaze is steady and clear. "Angela, I'm never going to marry you. And you don't want to marry me."

She bites her lip and the mask slips. Her eyes fill. "I'm sorry," she whispers.

"Sorry for what?"

She blinks rapidly, eyelashes flashing, her voice low. "If I don't do this, he's going to ruin Charlie."

"Who's going to ruin Charlie?"

Her eyes flick to the window behind me.

178

When I turn, there are paparazzi snapping photos. I shake my head and turn back to her. "What is this?"

She covers my hand with hers and leans closer. "I have to protect her. You should check on Bethany. I think your dad fired her this morning."

"What?" I pull away and stand.

She speaks loudly enough so the press standing outside can hear. "I can't believe you're doing this to me!" Then she stalks out the door.

A little dramatic, but if the flashing camera lights are any indication, it doesn't matter. People will eat it up.

None of that matters. Who's going to ruin Charlie? Dad? Did someone find out about them? I have to call Bethany.

I stalk to the elevator as quickly as possible, waving off the concerned look the security guy gives me.

Once I'm in the elevator I call Bethany, but it goes to voicemail.

Worry niggles at me.

Dammit, Dad.

He's next on the list and he answers right away.

"I'm not marrying Angela Sinclair." Might as well cut right to the point.

"You don't have to marry her. She's a pretty girl, just date her for a bit until this deal goes through."

"I can't date Angela. I'm dating someone else." And so is Angela, but I'm not getting into that right now.

"Look, Son, I know you think you like Beth but she's not for you. You have to suck it up and do this for the good of the family business."

I make it back to my apartment and shut the door with a hard thunk. "What is it with you and this business?" I explode. "You don't need the Sinclairs. It's not like we're suffering. You want me to do something that makes me unhappy just to make a few extra bucks?"

"We're talking millions here, Brent."

179

"What does it matter? We *have* millions. You're seventy-six years old. You can't pack up all that money and take it with you when you're gone."

He doesn't even hear me. His voice rises. "What does it matter to you? I'm asking you to take a pretty girl out for a couple months and you're acting like it's this big hassle. I'm talking about our family legacy, getting the Crawford name into households everywhere. It will live forever."

With my free hand, I pick up my old football from where I left it on the couch and squeeze the firm leather with my fingers. "I don't care about any of that. I care about my life, right now. I found someone, someone important, and I'm not going to ruin it."

There's a long pause. "You can't screw the help your whole life."

"It's not like that." I swallow. "Did you really fire her?"

"You're damn right I did."

"She is the best thing that happened to that place since Marc left."

He doesn't even bother acknowledging my statement. "I know what it's like to want to chase tail around the office all day, believe me."

"I'm not chasing her. We're together. Don't you understand? I need her. She's different."

He scoffs. "They're all good pretenders until they accidentally get pregnant and then she's got you by the balls and the bank account for eighteen years. At least Angela knows the score."

I slam the football against the wall in frustration. "You're not listening to me."

How can I get him to take me seriously? The phone beeps in my ear.

"I've gotta go. Roger is calling." I hang up before he can say anything else, taking a second to take a few deep breaths and pick up my ball from where it rolled on the floor.

He doesn't understand.

Money isn't important. Fame isn't important. What's important is right now, this moment, being with the people I love . . . making memories. My eyes fall shut.

Life is short. I can't make him see that, though. He has to see it for himself. Just like I had to.

I answer the other line. "Hey, Roger."

"Brent. We have a problem."

"What is it?" *What now?*

He sighs. "I just got a call from a friend at *Stylz*. They're running an article tomorrow about you having some kind of terminal heart condition. Is that true?"

Said organ thumps in my chest. "What? How . . . ?"

"What's going on?"

Shock forces me into silence. Someone spilled. But who? My hand flexes around the football and I stare down at the worn leather. "It's not necessarily fatal, but they're not exactly wrong, either. Who's the source?"

"I don't know. They're anonymous and apparently have some kind of recording of you talking about a heart problem and . . . there's no easy way to say this but they have you talking about not being able to get it up. I tried to get them to trash the story, but there's no way to stop it. They paid handsomely for the information and they're running it no matter what."

I shake my head. "That's . . . what?"

The only people who know the whole story are my doctors and Bethany, and she wouldn't.

Dad just fired her, a little voice in my head pipes up. *And she needs the money for her mom.*

No.

"Is it true? About your heart, I mean. Honestly, bud, we all have that other problem sometimes and it's nothing to be ashamed of."

"I was going to tell you. I'm having surgery in three weeks."

"We'll have to figure out how all of this affects your career. Is this why you've been avoiding signing the contract?"

"Yeah." But right now, I don't give a fuck about my career. Someone betrayed me. And the sinking feeling in my stomach is pointing to the only person I've given the power to completely destroy me.

My father's words ring in my mind.

I shut my eyes but it doesn't stop them from replaying in my head.

They're all pretenders.

No.

No.

Not Bethany. She's a terrible liar. She wouldn't do that. Images flash into my mind from this morning, staring into each other eyes, laughing in the sunlight. We were so connected.

I think about Bella. Marissa. Even Gwen. Maybe I'm the one who can't be trusted. Can I trust my own instincts?

"Is there any way to find out who this anonymous source is?" Because despite the evidence, despite my father's claims, despite my past, I don't believe Bethany would do this.

"I can try. I'll talk to my friend at the magazine. I doubt they'll spill, but I might have other ways to track them down." Roger's voice is gentle but firm. "Brent, this is a huge thing to keep under wraps for as long as you did. You signed a health statement at the end of last season. The team could sue you. Besides all that, I need you here as soon as possible. We'll have to set up something before this article runs, put our own spin on it."

"I'll be there as soon as I can." I hang up on him and then silence my phone.

I don't know how long I stand there, trying to breathe around the ache in my chest. It could be minutes, it could be an hour. This is it, the end of my career.

There's a knock at the door and I know who it is. There's only one person security allows up without calling first.

I open the door and she walks right by me, like she belongs here. Like it's any normal day.

"Ugh, today has been killer." She hangs her purse on the stand by the door, then she grimaces. "Bad choice of words. Don't freak, but Mr. Crawford fired me, for reals this time, because he saw those pictures of us . . ." She trails off as she takes in my expression and then reaches for my hands. "Are you okay? What's going on? Is it your heart?"

She's so concerned. So guileless. Her eyes are clear and open, the emotion written all over her face. This can't be a ruse. It can't be.

But I have to ask. Because there's still that inkling in the back of my mind, that "what if" that can't trust anyone. If she did do it . . . well, I wouldn't even care.

The realization stuns me.

I would understand, given what she's gone through, but I need to know for sure. I want her to be able to tell me everything. Anything. Good, bad, indifferent, shameful. All of it.

I care more about her than I do about my career or reputation or . . . anything else.

Her hands still in mine, I tug her into my chest and I'm finally able to breathe. "I got a call from Roger. There's uh . . ." I shake my head, clearing it. "Someone at *Stylz* got ahold of information about me. About my medical condition. They're printing an article tomorrow.

183

They know everything. About my heart. About the side effects from the medication. All of it."

She pulls back to look up at me, her mouth popping open. "They . . . what? How?"

I keep my eyes focused on her face. "I hate to even ask, but do you know anything about it?"

Her brows crawl up her forehead. "You think I told them? Why would I do that?"

I rush to explain. "I would understand if you did. I mean, my dad did just fire you. And I know what you're going through with your mom. And it's just, there's no one else who knows—"

"You think I would sell you out for money?"

"No. I mean, not entirely."

She steps back, away from me, and when I try to follow she holds a hand up to stop me. "First your dad fires me for putting you—for putting *us*—before him and my job, and now you are accusing me of using you for money? Don't you think I would have taken you up on your offer to help yesterday if that was the case?" Her voice rises as she speaks.

This is not going how I imagined. "I don't think you would betray me like this, but I just had to ask. No one else knows."

"Your doctor knows." Her arms cross over her chest.

My jaw clenches. I rub the back of my neck. I know she's had a bad day, but she's not the only one. "My doctor could lose her license. What do you have to lose?"

She blanches and goes pale.

I immediately regret the words. "Bethany, I didn't mean—"

"Maybe I should leave." She walks back toward the door, grabbing her purse from the stand.

"Please don't." I follow her, wanting to hold her, wanting to convince her I didn't mean it, but when she turns to face me, her expression is closed and guarded. I try once more. "Can we talk about this?"

"I think I need some space." Her breath hitches on the words. She won't meet my eyes. She pulls something from her bag and, instead of handing it to me, places it on the table in the entryway.

With a whisper of sound, she's out the door, shutting it gently behind her.

I walk over to the table and pick up the object she left behind. My watch. My super-expensive, six-thousand-dollar watch. I must have left it at her apartment.

Crushed with the weight of the last half hour, I slide down the wall to the floor, gripping the watch in my hand.

How can a day that started so beautifully twist so quickly into hell?

My chest tightens with pain. I choke back the tears that threaten to overwhelm me.

There's no time to rail at the unfairness of the universe. I have go see Roger and fix this mess. But my heart isn't in it. My heart just walked out the door.

Chapter Twenty

Courage doesn't mean you don't get afraid. Courage means you don't let fear stop you.
–Bethany Hamilton

Bethany

People always use the same old adages when you're going through a breakup.

He wasn't good enough for you.

There are other fish in the sea.

This, too, shall pass.

Those people are morons.

Brent *is* good enough for me, when he's not being an idiot who thinks that I could betray him. And there might be other fish in the sea, but none of them are him. And time heals nothing. It just makes the ache less acute.

But this is why I'm glad my friends are not those people.

"Did you watch the press conference?"

"I couldn't. It hurt too much. I'm still angry."

"He looks like a shit sandwich," Freya says, trying to make me feel better.

"If a shit sandwich was also slang for a hot-ass football player," Ted says.

We're video chatting. I'm on the couch in my PJs and Ted and Freya are together on the other end of the call, squeezed into the frame of my laptop.

"You're not helping, Ted." Freya nudges him with a shoulder and rolls her eyes at me.

"What? It's true. He would look good covered in dirty baby diapers. Bethany, you look like balls."

"I feel like balls. Tiny, sensitive, lumpy balls."

And Brent hasn't even tried to call me. Not once. I mean, we didn't really break up, did we? We just had a fight. A fight that is all his fault and he hasn't even called to apologize. Or come over.

"He did look tired," Freya says.

Ted snorts. "Well, he's dying, so I guess that will do it to you."

"I can't believe he has this horrible thing and you knew and somehow it got leaked. Who do you think told?"

"I have no idea. I just know it wasn't me."

"Well. We believe you. You're a crap liar."

"I know!" The words are punctuated with my righteous anger. Righteous anger that has spiked and deflated a million times over the last few days. "Brent knows that, too, and still he thinks I would do something like this. For money. Look at me. I haven't dyed my hair in six months, I'm wearing a dirty shirt, and I'm eating expired ramen. If I had sold his story for money, I wouldn't be sitting here like this, now would I?"

"Are you going to move back home?" Freya asks.

"No. I have a job interview tomorrow. I'm not giving up. I sublet this place from Gwen and promised to stay a year. I did send her an email to give her a heads-up, just in case. But I can't leave now."

Negative thoughts swirl in my head like crap down the sewer. What if I can't find another job? What then? It's not exactly easy in the Big Apple, thousands of people arriving every day, searching for their dreams. What do I have to offer?

187

This is the same thought that's been plaguing me about Brent. *What do I have to offer?* Nothing.

No wonder he hasn't called.

"I know how you can feel better." Freya holds up one finger and sticks it into a hole created by her other hand. "I won't even judge you. You've earned it for reals."

I laugh. "You know, I actually haven't slept with anyone in over a year."

"Right. Like you totally didn't go home with that guy after that concert downtown last year."

"I did go home with him. I slept on his couch. He was too hammered anyway. I drove him home and he passed out."

Freya blinks slowly. "You're being serious."

"Why would you do that?" Ted asks. "Why not just go home?"

Here it is. I have to tell them the truth. "There's something I should tell you guys."

"Oh my God. You're pregnant," Freya gasps.

"What? No."

"You're an alien."

"Freya, focus." Ted smacks her on the arm.

"My mom is an alcoholic. Like a bad one."

They share a glance and then look back at me. "Yeah. We know."

I rock back on the couch. "You know?"

Freya leans toward the computer, her expression softening. "It was pretty obvious that one time I tried to bring you chicken soup when you were sick. She kept yelling, 'Hi ho, Silver,' because I brought the bowl with the black and white cow print."

Ted laughs and then claps a hand over his mouth. "Sorry. Not funny. We didn't say anything because we knew you were embarrassed and didn't want to talk about it. So we just called you a slut to make you feel better."

"Well. I was a slut in college."

Ted nods. "Yeah so was I."

"Not me," Freya says.

"Prude," Ted and I say at the same time.

We dissolve into giggles.

I want to hug my computer screen. Then I do.

"Ew, boobs," Ted says.

I pull back. "I miss you guys."

"We miss you, too, skank face," Freya says.

~*~

The next day I'm flying around the house getting ready for my interview. There are clothes everywhere. I'm half-dressed and panicking.

I'm going to be late.

I've finally settled on an outfit and I'm buttoning my shirt when there's a knock at the door.

"Hey, Natalie."

She's standing in the door in surprisingly bird-free clothing, black T-shirt and dark jeans, with a sheepish expression. "Sorry to bug you. Can I use your bathroom real quick? Martha's been in ours all morning and I really have to go."

"I'm running late, but go ahead."

"I can lock the door as I'm leaving."

"No worries, I'll wait." I turn to grab my laptop case, throwing a résumé in the pocket.

"Well, you don't want to be late and miss out on the job."

My hands still on the zipper of my bag. "How did you know I was late for an interview?" I turn around and face Natalie. I'm sure I didn't mention it. I haven't seen or talked to any of my neighbors in days.

Just like I'm pretty sure I never mentioned my love of tater tots to her. Or to Steven and Martha.

Our eyes lock and then the pretty brunette smiles.

It's not a nice, easygoing, *you're so funny* smile, it's an *oops I screwed up and now I want to kill you* smile.

Bad news.

Tense energy crackles between us like lightning about to strike.

I spin on my heel and race for the door but the heels I'm wearing slow me down. A hard yank on the back of my head jerks me off my feet. I crash hard on my back, the air knocked out of my lungs.

Natalie stands over me.

"I wish there was another way. This is my last chance to search. I really wish you hadn't lost your job. Then you wouldn't be here and none of this would be happening."

Like this is my fault?

Bitch.

I can't talk yet, still struggling to get air in my lungs. She has something in her hands and my eyes flick to it. It's the lamp.

Oh no.

Chapter Twenty-One

If you make every game a life and death thing, you're going to have problems. You'll be dead a lot.
–Dean Smith

Brent

I move through my life on autopilot. Numb. Exhausted.

Even spilling my guts at the press conference was a fog. I simply read a script Roger gave me. Roger spins it in a very effective "woe is me" way, garnering sympathy from everyone. A flood of well-wishes and emails came in right away. Now the entire world knows. About my heart, my mom, the surgery . . . my impotence. The fact that I won't be signing a contract with the New York Sharks. The fact that I won't be playing ball in the foreseeable future at all.

The press immediately asks questions about Bethany and Angela.

I can't even fake a smile.

No comment.

In the days following the conference I finally call my brother and leave him a message, then he calls me back when I'm busy with doctors' appointments.

Apparently, Bethany and Gwen talked.

"Dude. We're in the middle of Nepal and I won't be able to call you again until tomorrow." Marc releases a gusty

sigh. *"Answer your phone. We need to talk. I love you. I want to kill you for keeping something like this from me."* He yells something in another language into the background before coming back on the line. *"Just, please answer your phone if you can."* Pause. The sound of wind in the background. *"Gwen talked to Bethany. She might have to move. She was a mess. She wouldn't tell us everything. Just . . . call me. Okay? I'll talk to you soon."*

I've let Roger handle all the fallout. I've been avoiding everyone and everything. Again. The thing I swore I wouldn't do anymore? I'm doing it.

It's time to man up and be the one to reach out.

"Hey, Dad."

"Brent." His voice is cool.

"I'm sorry I didn't tell you."

He must be in the car. Honking and the hum of traffic echo in the background.

But I don't hear what I want. Words, from him. Not that I should have expected anything. He's never been the best fatherly figure. Marc was more of a dad than he ever was.

Still. He's family.

"I'm sorry about the deal and Angela and everything. I had to make a decision for my health and future. I'm going to live my life the way I choose and you can be a part of it or not. I hope you choose me. I love you, Dad. Marc does, too. We both wish you would love us more than the company. When you figure out what's really important, if you ever do, please call me. Until then, I can't be a part of your life."

He's still not speaking. I wouldn't even know he heard me if not for the small hitch in his breathing.

"I'm having surgery in two weeks. I'll be at Mount Sinai. I'll . . . text you the details." I hang up and take a deep breath.

I would be shocked if he cared enough to be there.

I'll never understand my father. But it's okay. I don't need to cater to his whims anymore and the relief is instant, overwhelming, and . . . sad.

Sad for him, for me, for everything.

And there's only one person I want to share it all with. I scroll through my contacts, thumb hovering over Bethany's name. She must have gotten ahold of my phone at some point. She put "Bethany Nacho Beyotch Connell" as her contact name. I smile and shake my head.

Before I can click the button, the phone rings.

Roger.

"Hey, Roger."

"We got some information on the person who sent your details to the press."

"And?"

"The money was transferred to an account for Natasha Furmeyer. It might be an alias but do you recognize the name?"

I sit up, blood rushing from my head.

"Furmeyer?"

Steven's girlfriend.

Natalie.

Natasha? I rub my head. This doesn't make any sense.

Why would Natalie be selling my secrets to the press and how would she . . . ?

The intruder. The strange noises. The fact that someone had access to Bethany's walls. Was it her this whole time? Did she overhear my conversation with Bethany at her apartment?

And that means Bethany . . .

"Shit."

"What's going on, Brent?"

"I don't know. Hopefully nothing. I have to go."

I hang up with him and call Bethany.

It goes to voicemail.

My stomach is churning.

I pull up the camera app.

There she is. At B's door. I check out the time stamp. Two hours ago. No movement in or out since.

"Fuck!"

I run.

Chapter Twenty-Two

Pepper spray first, apologize later.
–Georgia Hardstark
My Favorite Murder episode 44

Bethany

My head hurts.

So does my neck. And my arms. And my legs. Also my wrists. I hurt everywhere. Even my nose hairs are aching.

Something is banging.

Not this again.

I blink my eyes open against brightness. All of the lights in the apartment are on.

Natalie is down the hall, ripping the wall next to the closet to shreds with a sledgehammer.

I can't move my arms. I'm sitting in one of the wooden dining room chairs, arms strapped behind me and held together by something I can't see. My hands are numb. I wiggle them and test the restraints but I can't tell if I'm making any progress.

"What are you looking for?" I ask.

She ignores me and keeps wrenching.

"If you're searching for something specific, maybe I can help you."

"Shut up. This isn't a movie. I'm not telling you anything." She goes back to pulling apart the drywall.

Dammit. What am I supposed to do with an atypical villain?

Think, Bethany, think!

I'm obsessed with true crime. I'm practically an expert on how to get out of untenable situations.

I wrench against the restraints more. They're too tight. I can't get out of them. But the chair is pretty flimsy. Maybe I can get her distracted enough to stand and fall backward, break the chair.

What the hell is she doing here? How can I distract her?

Sam said an old Mafia dude lived here and hid something.

It's worth a shot.

"Are you looking for that old lockbox?"

Banging stops. Natalie leans out of the wall, eyes locked on mine. "Box?"

"Yeah. I found it in the cranny in the closet when I first moved in."

Her eyes narrow.

She grips the hammer tighter in her hand and stalks toward me. "Where is it?"

I've hit a nerve. Jackpot.

"Untie me and I'll show you."

"No. Tell me where it is, then I'll leave and send Steven to untie you when I'm out of the country."

Damn her. I have to get her out of the apartment long enough to try and break out of this shit.

Time. I need time.

"I put it down in storage. I thought maybe it belonged to the person I'm renting from."

"Where's your storage key?"

"In my purse."

Before she leaves, she grabs a roll of duct tape and approaches me with a determined stride.

"No." I try to avoid it, twisting my head from one side to another, then back and forth until she basically crawls in my lap and forces me to stay still long enough to slap the tape on.

Bitch.

As soon as she leaves, I'm wiggling. I have to get out of this chair. I need to break out of these bonds before she realizes I'm lying and comes back with something worse than tape.

I strain and huff against my bonds. This bitch is good at tying knots. Fuck her.

It takes about two minutes to get down to the basement. Maybe another five to find the locker and discover there ain't shit in there but some old boxes of clothes Gwen left behind.

Then another two minutes to come back up and murder me. Probably less because she's gonna be pissed and running.

That's nine minutes.

I jerk against the bonds.

Tears of frustration fill my eyes and I blink them away. I don't have time for emotions right now. I need to get out of here. There's still so much I need to do with my life. I can't let it all be taken away by a seemingly nice brunette with a sledgehammer. I want to see my mother get sober. I want to see my friends . . . and Brent at least one more time. I want to get an awesome job and tell Mr. Crawford to shove his misogyny up his ass.

Someone stomps down the hall.

How much time has passed? I have no idea.

Oh shit.

Chapter Twenty-Three

Always make a total effort, even when the odds are against you.
–Arnold Palmer

Brent

For more than a year now, I've been tempting the fates, knowing my heart could stop, just like that. Snap. Gone in a blink.

I haven't cared that the exertion of playing out on the field or in practice could be exacerbating my condition. I've been a professional at denial. But not once in all this time have I been actually scared my heart would stop in my chest.

Until now.

I can't get to Bethany's apartment fast enough.

My heart is racing, breaking away every time I think about the fact she's in trouble and I let her down.

I call the police on the way, asking for someone to go because she could be in danger.

Could be in danger?

There's no time to explain the whole story. I hang up and park illegally because I don't care about getting towed, not when the woman I love is in trouble.

I don't even pause to examine that life-changing thought.

I love her.

It isn't really a thought at all, but a fact, a truth I sense down to my bones.

No one's buzzing me in and goddammit the super fixed the knob so I can't even break in. This is what I get for being demanding and overprotective. I buzz various apartment numbers until someone finally hits the buzzer.

Bypassing the elevator, I run up the stairs like her life depends on it.

The door is locked. I knock frantically. There are noises. Muffled voices. I don't have a key. I'll have to pay for a new door because nothing is going to stop me from getting into this apartment.

I brace myself on the other side of the hall and run, shoulder first into the door.

"Ughhgnnfdhdhsd." It hurts. They make it look so easy in the movies. I can't believe they lied to me.

I pull out my phone. It's been six minutes since I called the cops. They've got to be here soon. I have to think clearly. I need to figure out the best way to knock down a door. Feeling slightly ridiculous, but not wanting to keep ramming the door and break my shoulder for no reason, I google how to break down a door. It takes less than fifteen seconds to find the answer. A well-placed kick near the lock should do it.

It takes more than one kick, but finally there's a crack and the door busts open, the lock breaking out of the frame.

Bethany's there, tied to a chair, tape over her lips.

I immediately run to her, kneeling in front of the chair and reaching for the tape.

"I'm sorry," I breathe before I rip the tape off.

"Motherfucker!"

"Are you okay?"

"Yes. Hurry, untie me. She's coming back any second now."

I move behind the chair to wrestle with the ties at her wrist. "It's Natalie, right?"

"Yes. How did you know to come?"

"I saw her on the video. And Roger traced where the money went from the article—into an account owned by Natasha Furmeyer."

I move to her front and help her as she unties the knots at her feet.

"That name, why wouldn't she change it?"

Before I have a chance to answer, there's a voice at the door.

"I didn't have time." She's here. In the doorway, gun pointed in our direction. "I didn't think it would be this hard to find my uncle's stash."

"The cops are on their way," I say.

"I'll be gone before they get up here. Give me all the money you have on you."

"I don't have—"

"Empty your pockets!" she yells, moving into the living room, closer and closer.

"Okay, okay." I lift my hands before slowly reaching into my pocket for my wallet.

"Move faster!" The gun twitches and then she's pointing at Bethany. "Move faster or I shoot her."

She's shaking. Losing control.

My heart is pounding. I have to distract her from Bethany.

"I'm moving faster. Keep the gun on me, Natalie. Or should I call you Natasha?"

"Fuck you." The sound of the gun cocking makes my heart beat triple time.

It's still pointed at B.

Putting both hands up, I nudge Bethany with an elbow, hoping she'll be able to follow my lead.

I need to distract Natalie long enough for the cops to get here.

I gasp and stumble forward. "Pain," I grunt.

Natalie/Natasha watches me with narrowed eyes, a frown tilting at her lips. "Are you . . . faking a heart attack?"

"Not . . . faking." I fall to my knees, clutching my right arm. Shit. Wrong side. I switch my grip to the other arm.

Bethany lets loose an inelegant snort.

I glance over at her while falling to the floor.

She's laughing at me.

How can she be laughing at a time like this?

I collapse in a heap and slit my eyes up at Natalie. She's got one brow lifted.

This clearly isn't working.

A loud, strange sound fills the room.

Oo-eek, oo-eek.

"What the—" Natalie turns toward the door and Bethany uses the distraction to grab her wrist, tilting the gun at the ceiling.

The sound of the gun discharging thunders in the small space, making my ears ring and everything go *whomp whomp whomp*.

I have to help Bethany. I jump up to help her get the gun, but Steven's already there, yanking the firearm and immediately popping the magazine out and dropping the bullets to the floor like a pro.

You go, birdman. There's blood covering the side of his face from a gash near his hairline.

I move toward Bethany to help her restrain Natalie/Natasha but before I make it a step, the cops are in the doorway, guns drawn, all pointed at Steven.

Chapter Twenty-Four

You fail all of the time. But you aren't a failure until you start blaming someone else.
–Bum Phillips

Bethany

Two hours later, we're still talking to the police — who didn't shoot Steven, incidentally — but there was lots of shouting and gun pointing and mass confusion until someone recognized Brent as the tight end for the Sharks.

Then things immediately calmed. It's amazing what celebrity status can do.

It took a while for them to figure out what happened, but the video from the front door helps verify our story.

They still give Steven suspicious looks and I can't blame them. I mean, that mustache.

The weird *oo-eek* sound was a birdcall, which Steven used to distract Natalie. Apparently he's also been in a gun club, which is how he knew how to disarm the weapon.

Over the course of the police's questioning, we put together the rest of the story and pieces from the past couple of months.

Natalie's mobbed-up uncle had left his stash somewhere in the apartment building. He'd also left some debts to some real bad people and Natalie needed to pay them off or they would break her thumbs or do whatever it is mobsters do to people who don't pay up.

Natalie had obviously been using the dumbwaiter entrance for access to my apartment. She'd also been using Steven for access to the building. She'd originally thought the loot was stashed at Martha's but then realized it may have actually been in the neighbor's. A.k.a., mine.

The other night when I ran into them coming off the elevator and they left to stay at Natalie's, she waited until Steven was sleeping to sneak back and break in, knowing I was here alone and knowing Steven sleeps like the dead. The goal was to scare me away so she could have more time to search in my apartment without me present and calling the cops.

She was in the walls and heard Brent and I talking— she even recorded bits of the conversation. She was getting more and more desperate for money ever since the super had blocked off the dumbwaiter entrance and I had a camera installed.

She used her recording to get money from *Stylz*, enough to hold off the people after her, but it wasn't enough to keep them away for good.

Desperation made her a bit crazy. She tied up Martha, conked Steven over the head, and left them in Martha's apartment before coming over and tying me up.

The cops do a thorough search of my closet and walls where Natalie was digging, but there's nothing.

It could have been cleared out by a maintenance man or former tenant at any point over the last forty years. Who knows?

By the time the dust clears, it's only Brent, Steven, and myself left in the chaos of the apartment. The door is broken, the closet is busted, and there are bits of wall and drywall dust everywhere.

"Steven. Thank you for everything," Brent says, shaking his hand.

"I should have known better than to date someone I met online," he says. "I have to check on Grandma Martha. Bethany, if you need anything, we'll be right next door."

"Thanks, Steven."

He leaves and then it's just me and Brent.

"You can't stay here." He's eyeing the front door, which is not only busted without a lock, it's also covered in police tape.

"I know."

He helps me pack a bag. We need to talk, but I don't know where to start.

He must feel the same because we leave the apartment in silence and drive over to his building.

Once we're there, Brent makes tea. The adrenaline rush has dissipated and now I'm brimming with exhausted confusion.

We sit at the dining table, tea in hands, unspoken words hanging in the air between us like a lingering rain cloud. Where do we begin?

Finally, he places his mug on the table with a quiet clunk and shifts his knees in my direction. "I'm so sorry."

"No." I shake my head and put my mug next to his. "I'm sorry."

"I shouldn't have questioned you. I knew better. I did. I do."

"You had every right to ask." I clasp my hands in my lap. I want to reach for him, but I don't want to make the first move. Why did he wait so long to apologize? Did he change his mind about me? About us?

His hands move and for a flickering heartbeat of a second I think he's reaching for me, but instead he picks up his mug from the table.

"I want you to know, I'm pissed at Dad for everything he did. Not just to you, but how he's treated me and Marc. I'm not talking to him anymore. Also . . . I'm having surgery in two weeks." His words are rushed, like he needs to push them out as quickly as possible.

"That's good, Brent. I'm really proud of you." Does he want me to be there? Does he need my support? I search his eyes, but he shifts them down to his lap.

The questions simmer on the tip of my tongue, but I'm too scared to spit them out. What if he says no? He didn't come over tonight to start things back up, he came over to save me from a psychopath. Would he have come if not for Natalie?

I want to go to him. Lean on him. Tell him all about how I'm looking for jobs, unload the stress of getting Mom into rehab. And I want to comfort him, too. Support him during his dark time.

He glances at me and then away. He fidgets with his mug, picking it up, putting it down again. Then he takes a sip. He doesn't speak. There's no real indication he would welcome anything more from me.

And that's fine.

Maybe I need time to think over whether we're really good for each other or if we were leaning on each other for unhealthy reasons. Because of his heart, because of my mom.

Maybe it would be a good thing, just for a little bit, to see if we can stand on our own.

Chapter Twenty-Five

The only way to prove that you're a good sport is to lose.
–Ernie Banks

Bethany

I found a job. It's not the best job in the world. The pay is shit. I'll make enough to cover rent and little else. But it's something. At least I can get Mom into rehab for the next six months. I'll worry about how to pay for it later.

It's a beautiful day outside, the first real nice spring day in April, and I'm using the opportunity to stain my new door. The window is open, letting in the sun and air.

I'm sitting on the floor inside my apartment, getting the bottom panel, when there's a gentle knock on my doorframe.

It's probably Steven. He's bringing me some pamphlets on some rare bird found in Central Park, the Kirtland's warbler. We've gotten closer since the whole thing with Natalie. We can both use a friend.

"Did you already find the . . . ?"

My voice trails off when I see who's standing in the doorway.

Mr. Crawford.

He looks completely out of place in his expensive suit and his slicked-back hair. He makes the walls look even grungier than normal.

My mouth is agape with shock.

I click it shut.

"You want to come in?"

"Want is a strong word."

A startled laugh escapes me. "Come on in."

He steps into the apartment.

I watch while he eyes the stained carpet and shabby drapes.

"Can I get you anything?"

"No." Awkward pause. "I just wanted a minute of your time."

In the living room, I sit on the edge of the couch.

He's still standing in the small entry and I motion for him to take a seat on the chair opposite. He eyes it like it might bite his balls off before sitting gingerly on the cushion, crouched like he's ready to bolt at any second.

His face is drawn, his mouth curved into a frown.

"Mr. Crawford?" I prompt after a long moment of silence.

"I want to offer you a job."

I couldn't be more shocked if he had offered me a lap dance. "A job? My old job?"

"Not quite." Another pregnant pause while I wonder if I'm dreaming. "I want to offer you Marc's job."

I laugh. Man's got jokes.

He doesn't join me.

I blink. "You're not kidding?"

"Brent was right. You know what to do better than anyone else there. You care about the help . . . I mean, employees." He draws in a breath and releases it, some of the tension leaving his body. "Plus I need help finding my own replacement. I'm retiring. You won't even have to deal with me anymore."

"Is this one of those prank shows?"

He shakes his head. "It's not a prank." He rattles off a starting salary and benefits package.

I almost pee my pants.

"Come to the office tomorrow morning and we can negotiate your contract and go over expectations."

He stands and steps toward the doorway.

That's it?

"Wait." I stand in a panic.

He stops just in front of the doorway.

"Have you talked to him?"

He shakes his head.

"The surgery is next week."

"I know. He won't talk to me. And he's right to be angry. I lost both my boys because of my own stubbornness. Don't make the same choices I did."

"He loves you. If he didn't, he wouldn't be so upset. He just wants to know you care about him more than the business. You should tell him."

"Maybe I will."

With one last nod, he leaves.

I sink back down to the couch.

A job? A freaking major job. Do I want it? I might be good at it. Like, really good. And the first month's salary alone will pay for Mom's rehab. And a new place to live. A nice place with new furniture and clean walls.

Can this really be happening? I don't know whether to laugh or crap my pants.

Only one thing would make it perfect.

I pick up my cell phone and scroll through my contacts. My thumb hovers over Brent's name. *Brent Hottie McHotpants.*

Maybe he'll tell me to get lost, but then I'll know and I can move on.

No chickening out now. I push the call button, but it goes straight to voicemail.

Disappointment floods through me.

I'm sure he's busy, what with everything going on and surgery coming up.

I'll try him again later.

~*~

Later never happens. Between signing up for the new job—haggling with Mr. Crawford for something that actually involves a little work–life balance—and getting Mom into the rehab center, I don't have a moment to breathe until a week later.

Mr. Crawford and I are working late one night going over résumés in the conference room together when he drops it on me.

"The surgery is tomorrow morning."

Surprised, I look up from the paper in my hands to find him watching me from the other side of the mahogany table. "Are you going?"

"Are you?"

"I don't know."

His chin drops into his chest. "You should go. I'll cover things here."

"Are you—?"

He clears his throat. "What did you think about the third quarter sales reports from last year?"

I know he's avoiding the topic. But it's progress that he brought it up at all.

We don't talk about it again until we're leaving for the evening.

"So I'll see you Thursday?" he asks, brows lifted.

Tomorrow is Wednesday.

"Thursday," I agree.

It's kind of like Mr. Crawford has been replaced by an alien. Not the same person I used to work for.

Although he still makes sexist comments occasionally, and the staff is still terrified of him, he doesn't fire me every day and he stops himself when he realizes he's done something offensive. He's more subdued. Quiet, almost.

Bright and early the next morning, I show up at Mount Sinai and find the waiting room for surgical procedures. It's so early, there's hardly anyone there. Except one familiar couple.

"Gwen?"

"You made it!" She immediately wraps me in a hug before pulling back. "How are you? How is the apartment? Brent told us about all the madness. I can't even believe how much we've missed since we've been gone."

She moves back so Marc can give me a side hug.

"How is he?" I ask. I can't answer questions until I know.

"We haven't heard anything yet. They said it would take about four hours."

I nod, but I knew they wouldn't have info on the surgery yet. That's not what I was asking.

Gwen takes my arm and leads me to the seats they were occupying in the corner of the light blue waiting room. "He was nervous and I think he hoped you would be here before he went in."

"I didn't know what time. I tried to call him. I didn't know you guys were back."

She nods. "His phone has been off. Too much press and things going on, it was stressing him out more. He thought if you wanted to see him, you would show up at the apartment."

"I would have but . . . Mr. Crawford hired me to take over your old job." I nod to Marc. "He's retiring."

"Wait. *My* dad?" Marc interjects.

"Yeah."

"Dad is retiring? Are you sure?"

"Positive. He's really changed, Marc. I think everything that happened with you and now Brent woke him up."

"From the coma he's been in for the last thirty years," he mutters.

Gwen nudges him with her arm. "We should call him."

"You should," I say. "He thinks you all hate him."

Marc's mouth tilts and he nods. "Well, we kinda do."

"Maybe it's time to start over," Gwen says.

He kisses the side of her head. "You're the angel on my shoulder."

"Always."

Ugh they're so cute I want to barf.

I update them on everything from my viewpoint—since they probably already heard most of it from Brent—while they were gone, skimming over some of the more personal details involving Brent and I, but it's clear they already have an inkling.

After I answer their multitude of questions, Gwen tells me all about their time in Europe and the pics she got of some indigenous culture in Pakistan. By the time we've exhausted nearly everything we could possibly talk about, over an hour has passed but we still have time to wait.

As time ticks on, I get more and more anxious about how the surgery is going until I think I'm going to scream.

Finally, the surgeon emerges. She's all professional and unsmiling and fear pierces me. What if something horrible happened? But when we stand to greet her, her mouth finally moves into a small upward tilt.

"Everything went well. He's in the CV-ICU and they're removing the ventilation now. He's still under sedation but should be more awake soon. He won't be completely aware, but I know he would like to see a familiar face. Only one person can go back now."

My heart sinks. Marc should go. He's his brother. I'm just a friend. Barely that.

Marc nudges me. "She should be there."

"And you are?" the surgeon asks.

"Bethany," I say, glancing back at Marc in confusion.

"His fiancée," Gwen says.

My mouth pops open. "I'm—"

"You should take her back now just in case." Marc pushes me again and I shoot him a look.

The surgeon doesn't seem to notice the interaction, thankfully. "Right this way."

We're buzzed through a set of doors and then she leads me down a winding maze of turns and corridors to the room.

She leaves me in the white-walled room with Brent and a nurse who is pushing buttons on the machine next to the bed.

He's awake, gaze lowered, but his head lifts and when he sees me, he smiles. "Hey."

He's okay. I can see he's okay and he's going to be fine even though there are wires attached to him and a large bumpy bandage over his chest, but my eyes still fill with tears.

I move to the bed and grasp his hand.

His eyes are glazed, movements slow. His head trails down to our clasped hands and then back to my face.

He smiles sleepily. "You're an angel."

I chuckle. "Hardly."

"Sexy angel. Are you here for me?"

"Yes. I'm here for you."

"I'm so lucky. You're so beautiful. Who are you?"

The nurse laughs. "He's still pretty out of it."

"I can tell," I say.

"He might fall in and out of sleep for a bit. There's some water here if he gets thirsty. I'll be back to check on him in about thirty minutes. Push the button if he needs anything."

"Thank you."

She leaves and when I turn back to Brent, he's gazing at me with a light in his eyes.

"You're so stoned."

"Yeah," he murmurs. "That seems right." He stares down at our hands, rubbing the tops of my fingers with his thumb. He yawns. "Don't leave me again." His eyes flick to mine, serious for a brief moment before they fall shut and his body relaxes.

"I won't."

Chapter Twenty-Six

All of life is about fixing what you fucked up.
–Karen Kilgariff
My Favorite Murder minisode 4

Brent

My eyes are weighed down with sand. Grainy. Uncomfortable. My mouth is dry. My chest hurts. I blink my eyes open and stare at a textured white ceiling.

Everything is sore.

Light filters in from an open door around the edge of a light blue curtain.

I'm in the hospital.

Memories rush back. Surgery. Waking up in a different room.

Bethany.

Bethany.

I glance up and find her in the chair next to me, slumped over, one hand stretched out onto my bed near my fingers.

She's going to have a crick in her neck.

My hand moves over hers and I squeeze gently.

"Angry cinnamon bun." She jerks to wakefulness on a gasp.

I chuckle. "Having interesting dreams?"

She blinks at me. "You're awake."

"I'm here."

"How do you feel? Do you need the nurse?"

"Just some water would be great."

There's a cup on a tray nearby and she holds it up for me to take a sip.

"Better?"

"Better."

We stare at each other for a few long seconds. She looks tired and rumpled and her hair is sticking out in about a thousand directions. And she's still the most beautiful thing I've ever woken up to.

"Your dad was here," she says. "Gwen and Marc, too. They all went to get some food but should be back soon."

"Marc and Dad went to get food together? Willingly?"

"Yeah. Mr. Crawford is retiring."

"That's . . . what?"

She chuckles and her hand turns in mine, linking our fingers together. Is she being affectionate just because I'm in a hospital bed, or does it mean something?

"Yes. It's shocking, but your dad is really leaving the company. I mean, he's still an owner, but he's leaving the work part to others."

"But the company means everything to him."

"You and Marc mean more. And it was the only way he could show it. And he's giving me Marc's old job."

My jaw drops. "What? That's amazing, B." I squeeze her hand. "He couldn't have picked a better choice."

She bites her lip and her gaze dips. "I tried to call you."

"You did? My phone's been off."

"I know." Her eyes lift to mine. "Gwen told me. I wanted to tell you that . . . I miss you."

The lingering pain in my chest lightens with her words. "I miss you, too. I wanted to tell you that night, after the whole thing with Natalie. But I didn't want to

215

take advantage after what you had just gone through." It nearly killed me to stay quiet, to not take her in my arms and beg her to promise she'd never leave. But if she'd said yes, then woken up the next day and looked at me with regret? Or worse? "And I didn't want pity, or for you to take me back out of some sense of obligation."

Her head shakes at my words. "It would never be like that."

"Then can we start over?"

She shifts in the seat. "I don't really want to start over."

My heart plummets, hurt returning. I just had the stupid thing fixed, and now she wants to break it?

But then she smiles at me, her eyes watering, lips trembling. "I don't want to start over, because I want to pick up where we left off. You promised me a date. And I think there was something about twenty million orgasms?"

I bark out a laugh, then wince at the pain in my chest.

"Oh my gosh, I'm so sorry." Her hand moves to my arm.

"It's okay." The ache doesn't overshadow my eternal relief. "I feel like that number is slightly inflated."

Her brow lifts. "Are you saying you can't handle it?"

"Never." I lean forward, trying to get closer and the pain makes me grimace. "Eventually."

Her laughter is like rays of sunshine streaming through dark clouds. She leans into me, careful of my bandage, and kisses me gently on the lips.

"Hey, now, no riling up the patient." Marc's voice interrupts us from the doorway.

Bethany moves away, pink flooding her cheeks.

"You guys made up!" Gwen claps her hands together. "Come on." She grabs Bethany's arm. "We need to have some girl time so you can tell me all about it."

216

Why is she pulling Bethany out the door?

The explanation is in the doorway. Dad.

He won't meet my eyes and he shifts on his feet like he's ready to run.

Bethany and Gwen disappear out the door and Marc moves in closer.

"We have to stop meeting like this," he says.

I smirk. The last time all three of us were in the same room was at another hospital, after Marissa shot me in the arm.

He turns to the door and lifts his brows at our father, still hovering.

Finally, Dad steps into the room. "Brent. I'm glad everything went well with your surgery."

"Thanks, Dad."

Silence.

The squeak of sneakers on linoleum passes by the door. The machines next to the bed whirr and hum.

Marc clears his throat.

Dad steps closer to my bed and finally meets my eyes. "I'm sorry, Brent. I haven't been the best father but I want to be better."

I don't know what to say. I'm shocked into silence. Dad. Apologizing to me.

"That's . . . thank you."

"I know it's probably too late, but I would like to have a real relationship with both of you. I might be too old to learn new tricks, but I'm willing to try." He sighs and shakes his head. "Nothing was ever the same after your mother died. But that's not an excuse. I want to change. I'm a work in progress."

"Dad." I reach for his hand. "We all are."

His grip is firm, but his skin is thin and wrinkled, reminding me of how little time he might have left. His eyes are watery.

I clear my throat. "Especially Marc."

Marc flicks my leg. "Speak for yourself, little brother."

I roll my eyes. "I've been bigger than you since I was nine."

"I mean mentally and emotionally."

Dad chuckles. "Knock it off, you two." He takes a breath. "Promise we'll all get together?" He looks at me, then Marc, then back at me. "Somewhere other than a hospital?"

"I promise," Marc says.

"I promise."

~*~

"I'm kidnapping you." Bethany jumps on the couch next to me, bouncing on her knees, grinning, hair wild, wearing only a thin T-shirt and boy shorts, looking like every guy's wet dream. "Since you're my really real boyfriend and I can."

I smile. She loves referring to me as her "real" boyfriend.

It's been two months since the surgery. The recovery has been slow and painful. Frustrating since I'm used to being physically top-notch.

I'm still going to physical therapy, but they've cut it back and I'm doing more work on my own at home. I've been staying with Bethany at her place almost every night since Marc and Gwen are temporarily home. I've been helping her search for an apartment. And by help, I mean perusing ads and giving her tips on the best neighborhoods while she does all the legwork with Marc and Gwen.

I should be overjoyed. Leaping from buildings. On a high from life. But everything is a little . . . off.

And I don't really know why. I mean, part of it is the fact I still don't know if I will ever play ball again. I'm not where I was, physically, and won't be for at least a year. Maybe longer.

Roger terminated our contract. No bad blood, but there's no work for him to do for me. No more deals, no more sponsors. Not now.

And while the fear of death no longer looms over me, I lack purpose.

"Are you going to take me into the forest and murder me?" I lean forward to brush a kiss on her exposed thigh.

On top of everything else, Bethany and I still haven't had sex.

She's adorable. Sexy. Beautiful. Smart. Everything I could ever want. We've even prepared ourselves with birth control and clean bills of health. But . . . nothing.

I've stopped taking the beta-blockers. So why am I still broken? The doctor has assured me it's normal. I just underwent major surgery, not to mention trauma and depression from the end of my lifelong career goals. Stop putting so much pressure on yourself, she says. Stress makes it worse. But how can I not? Bethany doesn't act like it bothers her, but I think it does. I don't want to make her insecure, not about us, not after everything we've been through.

She lies on the couch, putting her head in my lap. "Close. I'm taking you to a beach house and I'm going to seduce you." She grins up at me.

I smile. "Sounds fun."

"Come on, lazy bum." She smacks my leg and bounces to her feet. "Let's get packed."

I don't fight her, but I know I'm not as excited as she wants me to be. I can't help it.

So like I've been doing for the past month, I follow along, riding Bethany's good mood like a stowaway.

She packs me and all our things—enough to last us a year—into the Panamera and then we're driving. It's a beautiful early summer day with my beautiful girl.

I even let her drive, though I know where we're going. She's been taking way too much pleasure in driving me around since the surgery.

Once we're out of the city, the greenery springs up like we've entered a different planet. We leave the concrete jungle behind and drive through the idyllic pastures and neighborhoods of Long Island.

The drive is mostly silent, peppered with Bethany singing Queen songs at the top of her lungs while I alternate between watching her and gazing at the passing scenery.

A few hours later, we arrive.

"We're here." Bethany puts the car in park.

We've finally reached the two-story grey clapboard house that backs up to the beach and smells like my childhood. The whoosh of waves crashing and the distant caw of seagulls filter through my open passenger window. I peer up at the house through the windshield.

It reminds me of chasing Marc down the beach, searching for shells, getting tan in the sun while Mom read trashy novels from the porch, yelling at us to put on sunscreen, dirt between my toes and bonfires on the beach. And laughter. So much laughter and freedom.

We grab the bags from the trunk and haul everything up the stairs and into the house.

Bethany chatters on about how the caretaker already made sure everything is clean and the kitchen is stocked with food. I half listen. I haven't been out here since before college, before my life became a blur of football and more football.

At this very moment, my former team is heading to training camp. Getting to know the rookies, working on pass plays and drills together before preseason officially starts in August.

Some of the furniture has been upgraded. I glance at the new flat screen TV on one wall, then my gaze wanders over the new dining set in the kitchen. New stainless steel appliances have replaced the old white clunkers, and there are shiny granite countertops.

There are pictures all over the walls of us kids . . . and Mom. My eyes trail over the memories. I drop my bags on the floor and walk through the living room straight to the back of the kitchen and out the sliding door.

The porch is smaller than I remember. The Adirondack chair Mom loved is still here. The bright blue wood is faded from weather and time.

I sit and stare out over the lapping waves, breathing in the salty sea air. Families are spread out up and down the shoreline, dotting the beach like freckles in the sand, the laughter of children on the breeze.

Bethany moves around inside. I left the sliding door open, and the sounds of her shuffling and murmuring to herself while she investigates the house make me smile.

She's the brightest part of my life. I love her so much.

Am I enough for her?

Familiar tendrils of hopelessness twine themselves around my body, tightening my shoulders. What if I don't ever find a purpose? And then I drag her down into my useless existence?

A breeze whips around me, tickling my nose with the scent of lemon and sugar. Memories of happy summers in this same sunshine settle around me like a hug.

Peace floods me, calming my thoughts and drowning out the despair, replacing it with a sense of hope and relief.

Emotion overcomes me. And I know. Down to my bones.

Everything is going to be okay.

A tension in my body releases. I sit there for I don't know how long, realizations hitting me with startling clarity, as if someone else is whispering truths into my ear, but one stands above the rest.

It will be okay.

If you're still breathing, then there's hope left.

I breathe deeply, trying to make sense of the moment, wondering if my mother is here, watching, helping.

"It's so beautiful out here." Bethany walks out the door and sits on the armrest of the chair.

I tug her onto my lap and she shrieks out a laugh. "It's not as beautiful as you." I pull her into me and inhale her wildflower scent. I've missed hugging her close to my chest. For most of the past two months, we were affectionate as much as possible, but we had to be careful of the incision site over my heart.

"Aww."

"Or as loving. Amazing. Wonderful. Smart." I sprinkle each word with a kiss to her neck, collarbone, shoulder.

She giggles, squirming on my lap. The movement sends a wave of heat into my stomach. Blood rushes south, my shorts tighten, and then . . .

"Let's get some food." She hops off my lap and tugs on my hands to get me out of the chair.

There's always hope. I don't put too much thought into it, though.

Because now I know, it doesn't really matter. Everything will be okay.

We go out to eat at a little café and then walk along the beach, laughing and talking. I can't stop touching Bethany. Over the past few months, she's become as familiar to me as my own body — if not more so. And yet, I can't get over the surprising softness of her skin or the comfort of her just being there.

We fall asleep, wrapped in each other's arms.

And in the morning, something is markedly different.

"Brent." The soft word whispers across my face.

"Hmmm?"

"Brent." Now louder.

My eyes blink open to find Bethany lying on her side facing me, mirroring my position.

Her wide eyes are pointed at my midsection.

I follow her gaze.

What she's staring at is apparent through the thin cotton of my boxer briefs.

I have an erection.

"It's the most amazing thing I've ever seen," she whispers.

I crack up.

"Stop laughing!" She smacks my arm. "You'll make it go away!"

"Come here."

I kiss her pout away and tug her closer. She melts into me, one leg going over my hip, pressing our bottom halves together.

The thin fabric of our underwear is the only thing between us. When she sighs into my mouth and I thrust against her, I almost explode with want.

"Brent," she gasps. "Too many clothes."

It's a rush to remove all the barriers between us, and when I thrust again, this time against her slick heat, it's too much. I'm like a teenage boy all over again.

Slowing down, I continue with gentle thrusts. Not entering, just teasing and working her into bliss, peppering my movements with soft kisses and drowsy gazes locked onto each other.

Right after she falls apart in my arms, I slide into her for the first time.

"I love you," she whispers, our eyes still locked.

"I love you. So much."

The distant numbness that had encapsulated me since surgery shatters into oblivion. It was all in my head. We've made love a million times in different ways over the past few months. Every time we touched or held each other, every soft-spoken word, every lingering gaze of affection . . . the *making love* part was already there. This is just one more page in our playbook.

The sensation of skin on skin, the feel of her around me, the gasp of our breaths and scent of wildflowers mixed with sex. I hold out as long as I can, but it's never going to be long enough.

When I explode inside of her, I practically leave my body behind on Earth. When I come to, Bethany is kissing me with soft brushes of her mouth. My cheek, my eyes, the corner of my mouth, my ear.

"We need to do that, like fifty million more times," she says, settling down in the bed next to me, her chin on my chest, a finger tracing my scar.

"At least." I shift to face her more fully. "We have time. Forever. If you'll take me for that long." The words fall out of my mouth without much thought but when I stop to examine them, they feel right and true.

"Wait. What?" Her head lifts up. "That's not a question, is it? Please tell me you're not asking like that right now. Like this."

"What's wrong with this?"

She gestures down to our bodies. "I'm naked."

"I like you naked. Would you rather I ask you to give me forever when we're at the scene of a horrible murder?"

"Oh my gosh yes!" Her eyes light up with excitement. "Wasn't there a famous murder in the Hamptons? Some rich guy? The wife did it. His place has gotta be nearby."

"We could do that but then we'd have to put on pants."

She grimaces. "You're right. Pants are the worst. Are you sure you want to tie yourself to someone crazy like me?"

"You're it for me, B. For the rest of my life." I pause to make sure she hears my next words. "Owl never want anyone else."

Her head throws back and she laughs. "I see how this is. You have to marry me. No one will love your bird puns like I will. Okay. Fine. We can get engaged. But this doesn't get you out of the hundred million orgasms. You still have, like, at least ninety-nine point nine million to go."

"Right. I'm on it. It's a good thing we have a lifetime to reach that number."

"You'll never *egret* it."

I swallow her laughter and proceed to cut my orgasm obligation down.

By at least a few.

The End

About the Author

Mary Frame is a full-time mother and wife with a full-time job. She has no idea how she manages to write novels except that it involves copious amounts of wine. She doesn't enjoy writing about herself in third person, but she does enjoy reading, writing, dancing, and damaging the eardrums of her coworkers when she randomly decides to sing to them. She lives in Reno, Nevada, with her husband, two children, and a border collie named Stella.

She LOVES hearing from readers and will not only respond but likely begin stalking them while tossing out hearts and flowers and rainbows! If that doesn't creep you out, email her at: maryframeauthor@gmail.com
Website: http://authormaryframe.com
Follow her on Twitter: @marewulf
Like her Facebook author page:
www.facebook.com/AuthorMaryFrame

Imperfect Series—All books are stand-alone and can be read in any order! With a guaranteed HEA!

Book One: Imperfect Chemistry – Lucy and Jensen
Book Two: Imperfectly Criminal – Freya and Dean
Book Three: Practically Imperfect – Sam and Gemma
Book Four: Picture Imperfect – Gwen and Marc
Book Five: Imperfect Strangers – Bethany and Brent

Extraordinary Series—Not stand-alone novels! Must be read in order!

Book One: Anything But Extraordinary
Book Two: A Life Less Extraordinary
Book Three: Extraordinary World

Made in the USA
Middletown, DE
23 November 2018